The Twins, the Pirates, and the Battle of New Orleans

Harriette Gillem Robinet

A Jean Karl Book
Atheneum Books for Young Readers

Books by Harriette Gillem Robinet

Ride the Red Cycle

Children of the Fire

Mississippi Chariot

If You Please, President Lincoln

Washington City Is Burning

The Twins, the Pirates, and the Battle of New Orleans

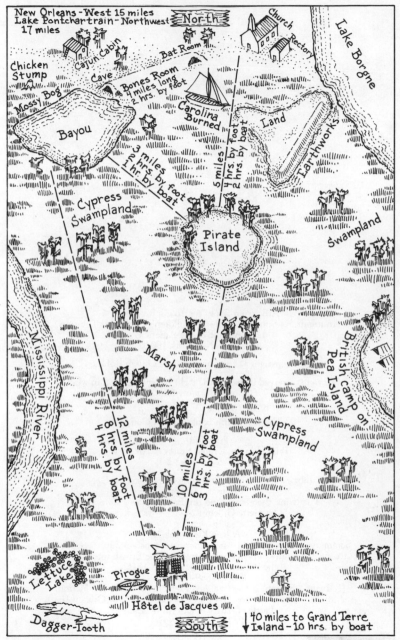

New Orleans - West 15 miles
Lake Pontchartrain - Northwest 17 miles

North

Church

Lake Borgne

Rectory

Chicken Stump

Cajun Cabin

Bat Room

Cave

Bones Room
1 mile long
2 hrs. by foot

Mossy Bog

Carolina Burned

Bayou

Land

Earthworks

3 miles
2 hrs. by foot
1 hr. by boat

5 miles
4 hrs. by foot
2 hrs. by boat

Cypress Swampland

Pirate Island

Swampland

Marsh

British camp on Pea Island

Cypress Swampland

Mississippi River

12 miles
8 hrs. by foot
4 hrs. by boat

10 miles
6 hrs. by foot
3 hrs. by boat

Lettuce Lake

Pirogue

Hôtel de Jacques

Dagger-Tooth

South

↓ 40 miles to Grand Terre Island - 10 hrs. by boat

Map by Rick Britton

Atheneum Books for Young Readers
An imprint of Simon & Schuster Children's Publishing Division
1230 Avenue of the Americas
New York, New York 10020

Book design by Angela Carlino
The text of this book is set in Goudy.

First Edition
Printed in the United States of America
10 9 8 7 6 5 4 3 2 1

Library of Congress Cataloging-in-Publication Data
Robinet, Harriette.
The twins, the pirates, and the Battle of New Orleans /
Harriette Gillem Robinet.—1st ed.
p. cm.
"A Jean Karl book."
Summary: Twelve-year-old Afro-American twins attempt to escape in
the face of pirates, an American army, and the British forces during
the Battle of New Orleans in 1815.
ISBN 0-689-81208-6
[1. Twins—Fiction. 2. Fugitive slaves—Fiction. 3. Slaves—Fiction.
4. Afro-Americans—Fiction. 5. Pirates—Fiction. 6. New Orleans (La.),
Battle of, 1815—Fiction.] I. Title.
PZ7.R553Tw 1997
[Fic]—dc20
96-22028

Dedicated to Stephen Robinet

This book is dedicated to our son, Stephen Joseph Robinet. When he heard that I wanted to research this story, he went out on a cold winter's night to the Left Bank Bookstore and bought a book he had spied earlier that day. The book was about Jean Lafitte and his Pirate Brotherhood.

Thus I began my research, and this book was born. However, this was just one instance of our son's constant encouragement and support. Thank you, Stephen.

chapter one

Stay in this cypress tree. I'll find a way to get that hen."
With that whisper, Andrew had scrambled across wet tree
roots to another tree in the swamp.

Frowning, Pierre crouched on a cypress branch.
Andrew, his twin, was now perched in a tree across the way
busy tying a rope.

Pierre gritted his teeth. Andrew didn't know what he
was doing. On a rope that long, he would swing into the
water. Pierre pointed and whistled a warning. Andrew
didn't look up.

Frogs and swamp insects chirped warnings too, that
December 1814 afternoon. Ducks and geese wintering in
the Gulf Coast wetlands discussed the plight of the twins in
steady quacks and honks.

Pierre wanted to yell at Andrew, but to be safe from
capture he had to stay silent. They were escaped slaves, trying to survive in the swampland long enough for their
father to free their mother and sister.

Both of them were dressed in green velvet jackets,
scarlet red sashes, black pantaloons, and white stockings.
They looked and dressed the same, Pierre thought. Both

had long, limp black curls and startling pale gray eyes, staring from earth-brown faces. Ghost eyes, their master the Marquis De Ville had called them. But although they looked alike, they never acted the same.

Andrew swung out on the rope that he had tied high in his tree. He looked, Pierre thought, like bait dangling on a fish line. The object of this was to swing across the deep water of a bayou to a place where they had seen a chicken. Andrew had whispered, "Brother, a hen will lay eggs to help us stay alive."

Pierre glanced down to where the waters mirrored the gray skies and dark clouds of December. A ripple crossed the water. Golden tan eyes slid rapidly toward Andrew. Pierre whistled to warn his twin.

Ignoring Pierre, Andrew swung again. The alligator lunged at him with a swoosh. Its dagger-sharp teeth tore off a black leather shoe with a silver buckle. Wavering on its tail the reptile stood in the water, then fell with a splash.

As Pierre watched, red seeped along Andrew's white silk stocking. Just as he had feared, that rope had been too long. Were the cuts deep? Would there be infection to drive his brother into fevers?

They had to stay alive! Jacques—their father who had helped them escape to the swamp—had left and hadn't returned. They might have to free their mother and little sister themselves.

Once again Pierre whistled to Andrew, a whistle they had used back at Chateau De Ville. Pierre had made up a private language of whistles to signal when they should meet each other. They had worked far apart on the estate, except when they had danced together for the marquis's guests. The whistles arranged stolen moments at midnight, because being with each other was forbidden.

Separating family members was the marquis's way of making his slaves helpless. Pierre had once heard him tell a lie to a woman to make her angry with her husband. Aunt Berniece had called it "Divide and conquer."

Andrew climbed higher on the rope, shaded his eyes, and smiled. That surely meant, Pierre thought, that Andrew's bloody foot didn't hurt badly. But then, Andrew was brave. Pierre both admired and disliked him.

Leaving the rope in the tree, Andrew gave up his chicken venture and scrambled across tree branches and down to reach Pierre's tree. He whispered, "About three miles or so to the east there's an island of oak trees in solid earth. I think we should go see it."

Pierre shook his head. "Why don't you just get the chicken and leave? We can make it back in the dark of night." From early morning they had traveled about eight hours away from Hôtel de Jacques—the swampland hideaway Jacques had built.

"No," said Andrew, frowning and glancing over his shoulder.

"We must get back. We're safe at our hideaway," Pierre said. "Who needs an island?"

"We do," said Andrew.

"Hôtel de Jacques is safe," Pierre said in a whisper.

"Not in a hurricane."

Pierre felt hairs rise on the nape of his neck. Was that true? Was Andrew thinking ahead for a change?

"The island's over there and we can reach it."

"But your foot's festering."

"My foot is fine."

"Let me see your wound." After looking, Pierre stripped off one of his own white silk stockings and wrapped Andrew's foot. Soon both old and new stockings were slippery with blood, and Pierre's hands were sticky and red. However, Pierre decided Andrew's cuts from the alligator's teeth seemed small. Feeling better, Pierre climbed down, rinsed his hands, and shook them.

Andrew tugged at Pierre's jacket and whistled. Anyone listening might have thought a tree frog chirped. "Follow me," Andrew said in a whisper.

Pierre jerked his shoulder from Andrew's grasp. It seemed foolish to go farther from their swamp home, but he knew he had to follow. Without his brother, he couldn't find his way back.

The swamp held danger from animals and danger from people. In the past week they had heard more people's voices, and more boats being rowed, than at any other time during their five or six weeks alone in the swamplands. Why did Andrew need to look at an island? Wasn't he being foolish?

On the other hand, thought Pierre, Andrew was the one who had invented a way to swing and splash through the swamp. And it was true, they needed different food. Catching a hen for eggs seemed a good idea. But who would be responsible for feeding that hen?

Walking on the toes of his hurt foot, Andrew moved off; afraid to remain behind, Pierre followed. They ran between cypress trees. They walked on tree roots and splashed across shallows. When the waters were deep and wide, Andrew tied a rope high in a central tree branch. First Andrew, then Pierre swung over open water. They left the rope safely hidden for the return trip.

Pierre was exhausted by the time they arrived at the island two hours later. And it was growing dark. Suppose someone was there? he thought. Had Andrew thought about that?

The island was about the size of a house and large garden. Surrounding the island was a ring of swamp oak and red swamp maples hung with Spanish moss. Trees in the center of the island had been cut down. Logs, chopped and split, lay haphazardly waiting to be burned. Clearly the island was used by people.

The people had been sloppy housekeepers, though. Rawhide trousers, peaked short-brim hats, white shirts, colorful sashes, scarves, and muddy boots lay tossed here and there.

Pierre and Andrew stared at each other. "Pirates," they said together, and Andrew grinned. He raced around poking in piles of clothes.

"Look," he called. He held up a ship's telescope, then tucked it in his sash. Gold bracelets fell from a pile of white shirts. Pierre dug up a gold doubloon with his wet shoe.

"There's a trunk," Andrew called, running toward it.

Pierre examined a pile of leather trousers, and red and yellow sashes. He lifted a string of pearls, then tucked them back under a yellow sash. "Andrew," he said, "this is dangerous. Let's get away from here."

Andrew held the trunk top open and whistled. Pierre saw the gleam of gold in the moonlight and ran over. Why would pirates leave gold unguarded? There were heaps and heaps of gold. Andrew ran his fingers through coins that clinked pleasantly. Some of the gold coins were Spanish, struck with the heads of King Ferdinand and Queen Isabella; others were French with heads of several kings named Louis.

"Gold to buy our mother and sister," said Andrew.

"It's pirate gold, and we aren't thieves," Pierre said.

"Lafitte's Brotherhood," said Andrew.

Nodding, Pierre glanced at his brother's leg. The foot had ceased dripping blood, but Andrew stood only on his toes. The heel must hurt. It was growing dark, and he tugged at Andrew's scarlet sash. "Let's go."

Andrew stared at the twilight. "We'll return to get that chicken and sleep in a cypress tree."

"Why?"

"I can't find our way back to Hôtel de Jacques in the dark." Pressing his lips together, Andrew frowned. With a stick he struck a rotten log that was growing mushrooms in honey-tan clusters. The log broke open. Sparks of yellow stuck to the stick, and the exposed wood glowed yellow.

"Fox fire," Pierre said.

"Suppose we make some glowing footsteps?" said Andrew with a mischievous grin. "Won't the pirates be surprised?"

"I think we ought to leave here," whispered Pierre. "Who knows when they'll come back?" He held his hand over one of the fire pits, but the stones were cold.

"Hurry then, Brother," Andrew said. "Help me." He passed broken chunks of glowing fox fire wood to Pierre.

Andrew was always telling him what to do, thought Pierre. But he had to smile when Andrew began making fox fire footsteps across the center of the island. Glowing footprints shone in the dark. Pierre made footprints that ran in a circle, then a second circle for a figure eight. Finally he caught his brother's red sash and pulled him to race to the water.

When they arrived, Pierre whistled a warning. He had heard a swishing sound. The boys stood as still as the tree trunks. Ahead of them a half moon lit the chilly swamp waters. Andrew's hands glowed yellow. Pierre made him hide them, and he shoved his own hands in his jacket.

Soon a longboat slid across the waters. A dog's chin rested on the side of the boat. The dog raised its brown ears and stared at the boys, but didn't bark. Four bearded men slumped in the seats. One, black of skin, scratched behind the ears of the dog. Another man, with head tied in an orange kerchief, rowed. As soon as the boat passed, Andrew pushed Pierre to climb up and swing out on the rope they had tied on the island.

When they had landed in marshy grass at the base of a lone tree, Pierre heard the pirates scream. One called: "Ghosts have visited!"

"Numskull fool, 'tis nothing but fox fire."

"Who walks in fox fire? Ghosts, I say."

Andrew giggled and Pierre smiled. So pirates were superstitious? That was interesting. It was something to think about as they scrambled back toward the distant bayou.

chapter two

When Pierre awoke at dawn, he saw Andrew tying a rope to try to swing across the bayou. Pierre felt stiff as a long-dead cat. When he glanced at his brother's foot, he noticed the blood had dried to dark brown.

Pierre crawled across tree branches to his brother. "I think we should go back," he said in a whisper. "This is dangerous."

"Did you hear that rooster crow all night?" Andrew asked. "There's a rooster and hens."

Pierre stared at Andrew. "A rooster crowed?"

"You slept well. Bring the sack. I know what I'm doing. I'll get a hen for you to feed."

That's what Pierre had been afraid of. He would be responsible for that hen. "But, Andrew," he said, "pirates are nearby. Let's not worry about a hen. If we leave now, we can reach Hôtel de Jacques before sunset."

"No. Swing after me." Andrew climbed down to grasp the rope. Exploring might be rally rousing for Andrew, Pierre thought, but the safety of Hôtel de Jacques was what they both needed.

Kicking away from cypress shrub, Andrew swung several times until he landed with a swoosh across the bayou onto the edge of a mossy bog.

Now it was Pierre's turn to swing out. He wound a large brown sack twice around his waist and tied it in front. When he saw Andrew sling the rope toward him, he hoped he could be brave like Andrew.

He had worked with women near the chateau, while his brother had worked with men in the field. Was that what made the difference between them? He clutched the line, crossed himself with a prayer, and in one mighty leap swung all the way across the bayou to the bog.

"*Sacré bleu,*" Andrew said in a whisper. "You made it in one swing, Brother." He raised his eyebrows.

Pierre smiled. I did, he thought. Andrew tried and tried first, but I made it in one swing.

A broken fishing pole lay on the moss. He jerked Andrew's arm. "Hurry, before someone sees us."

They ran splashing on wet moss until they reached drier land. Panting, they hid under a mighty live oak hung with heavy gray-green Spanish moss, ferns, bromeliads, and delicate white blossoms of ghost orchids.

Pierre closed his eyes and rested his forehead against a soft fern. He was tired and wanted to get back to safety.

"Brother," said Andrew, pointing, "I think I was right. There's that hen." Pierre felt his brother begin to untie the brown sack from his waist. When he opened his eyes, he saw that Andrew had his foot raised. It must hurt.

"Alligator bait!" he said softly to Andrew.

"Hen heart," said Andrew. "Now you creep over and grab her. I'll stand here under the tree and hold the sack."

"Is this stealing, Andrew?" asked Pierre before moving.

"Of course not. We need this hen. It's called staying alive. We're not robbing a henhouse."

The black-and-white speckled hen rested atop a tree stump that was shoulder high to Pierre. He covered her back with one hand and slid the other under her warm feathery breast. The bird barely moved. She was someone's chicken after all, and a pet at that. After he placed her carefully in the sack, he felt smooth eggs in that tree stump.

With a low whistle, he returned and handed four brown eggs to Andrew. They went into Andrew's pocket. "See how easy that was?" asked Andrew.

Moving out, Andrew stalked another hen and an uncooperative squawking rooster. They joined the first hen. Once in the dark sack, the chickens murmured sleepily. All they had wanted was one chicken, Pierre thought, now they had three. Would a crowing rooster make trouble? In the distance he thought he saw a cabin.

Andrew said, "I'll let you carry the sack, Pierre."

Sure you will, thought Pierre, as he slung the bag over his shoulder.

The sun rose over the wetland, and the day was suddenly bright. Fog and mists swirled around them like silvery silk veils. Pierre began to run, but Andrew limped slowly so Pierre stopped and waited for him.

At the water's edge Andrew used a dead tree branch to pull the dangling rope over, and they swung safely over the bayou to the cypress tree.

Ready to travel now, they picked up coils of rope, less than they had carried at the start because they had left rope in trees. Fog and mist concealed them as they began the long return trip. They traveled around trees, splashing between them. They found some rope they had already tied to use for swinging over deep water, but sometimes Andrew had to tie new rope.

He made a face when his foot accidently struck a tree, Pierre noticed. He had tended infectious wounds with old Dr. De Ville. Often he had watched soakings and poultices applied to draw out poison. He had also watched people die from gangrene—yellow pus oozing from infected cuts. He shivered.

Andrew must have sensed Pierre's concern. "If I die," Andrew said in a dramatic whisper, "I'll die free. That's worth more than a million gold doubloons." Pierre nodded.

A graceful black swamp snake waved before his eyes, then slithered down the tree in whose branches they were resting for a moment. Pierre leaned back and held his breath. As the snake slid into the waters, he leaned out to watch the waters part in widening circles and saw a boat that had appeared out of nowhere. He whistled a warning to his brother.

To the man in the boat below them the whistle may have sounded like one more bird call. The twins watched the man nail a paper to a tree, then row quietly away. Andrew slid off the branch to climb down, but Pierre held him back. "He might hear if you go down now."

"Let the man row farther," he whispered. He closed his eyes and lay his face into damp sweet-smelling Spanish moss until slowly Andrew squeezed his wrist. What had happened now?

chapter three

Below the boys a boatload of men glided in the swirling mists. They wore white pants. Their scarlet red jackets were difficult to see in the mist, but Pierre knew these were red-coats, British soldiers fighting Americans in a war called "Mr. Madison's War" after President James Madison.

Pierre took a deep breath. It had taken two years of fighting, but the war had finally arrived in the swampy out-skirts of New Orleans. Would the British burn New Orleans as they had burned Washington City last August? Would there be battles in the wetlands?

"Lieutenant," said one man in the boat, "how far are we going?"

"Devil knows where this band of murderers awaits us," said a deep voice. "Scum from French gutters. Cutthroats."

"Begging your pardon, sir, should we go on?"

Their lieutenant muttered, "We know Jackson's been warned. We'll need those cutthroat pirates who're familiar with this swamp. Never know when those Americans might attack."

Pierre froze like an icicle above the boat. His brother

stretched lightly. When the chickens murmured sleepily, Pierre wondered if the chickens would give them away.

He hoped Andrew still had those eggs. His stomach felt as hollow as a cave. They had finished a supply of cat-o'-nine-tail roots on this adventure. Cattail roots were filling, like rice or bread. When raw, they were crunchy; when cooked, they were chewy. But those they had brought hadn't lasted beyond noon yesterday.

With a curse the lieutenant ordered his men to row on. Pierre watched as the boat left wave after wave of gently sloshing water.

Andrew and Pierre stared at each other. Before Jacques had brought them to the swamp, General Andrew Jackson's men had arrived in New Orleans to prepare the city for a British attack. Now the British were here.

How many days had the two of them been in the wetlands? Pierre would have to count the notches he had cut each day after their father left. As soon as he got back, he would do that. If they got back. Pierre sighed.

Andrew seemed to sense what his twin was thinking. "Don't worry," he said in a whisper. "I'll find my way."

Pierre nodded. "Andrew," he said, "if Jacques hasn't come back, it's because he's most likely dead."

His words surprised him. He was saying what they were afraid to think. Neither of them had wanted to say it, he suspected, and now he had. It meant they might be responsible for their own lives now, and also for freeing their mother and little sister.

He glanced over his shoulder. The sun was higher and burning off the mist.

Andrew said, "I think you're right."

Pierre shivered and stared into the waters below. If Andrew agreed with him, it might be true. They had to make plans. He glanced at his brother. "What're you thinking, Andrew?"

"I'm thinking I'm hungry," said Andrew. He pulled out the four eggs and handed two to Pierre.

Pierre was disappointed. He had wanted to talk seriously with his twin, but he was also hungry.

And so they breakfasted on raw eggs, sucking from chipped ends. The eggs were refreshing, slipping easily down Pierre's throat. He licked his teeth and glanced at his red sash and tight black pantaloons. They were not dressed for swamp life.

The Marquis De Ville dressed the twins in French fashion and made them dance like court jesters to entertain his friends. In hours of practice a dance master taught them acrobatic leaps and dance steps so the marquis could show them off like trained poodles.

However, the marquis also taught them their "place" as slave boys. He kept them apart and often starved them for discipline. As a result both boys were thin, but muscular and agile.

Andrew pointed. "I think we go that way—southeast—but first I'll go for the paper." He swung over, whistled, and returned with the notice. With a frown he handed it to Pierre. It read:

Marquis François Jean Claude De Ville
demands return of twin slave boys, twelve years

old, stolen or runaway. Black hair with loose curls, brown of skin with pale gray eyes outstanding. One-thousand-dollar fine for aiding and abetting. One-thousand-dollar reward for return.

They read it over and over. Andrew whistled, and Pierre answered with a whistle. Pierre pointed to the word *stolen*. "They don't know how we escaped," he said. "They haven't caught Jacques, or they would say something about him."

"Many know our path," Andrew whispered.

"Jacques's path," said Pierre. "Not ours."

He remembered how surprised they had been that evening weeks ago when Aunt Berniece had kissed them, handed them a clothes bundle, and told them to walk to Lake Pontchartrain behind Chateau De Ville. Jacques waited for them behind a tree. He was tall and muscular, with brown skin and pale gray eyes like theirs.

Pierre had stared at his father. He couldn't remember the last time he had seen him. Isabel, their mother, had been gone three years. She had visited with Jacques, but the twins had only seen him from a distance.

"Remember me? Your father?" Jacques had asked. "I'm taking you to freedom. Into these bags then, and I'll tie both of you across this horse."

In November's purple dusk the brothers, tied in two sacks, had lain across a broad-backed horse. For hours they had galloped away. The dark sack had been a strange bed. The horse smelled of a barn and felt warm, but at every move Pierre had been fearful of sliding off.

Andrew had whispered, "Isn't this rally rousing?"

Pierre had answered "Yes," but he hadn't meant it. He heard his brother's even breathing when he fell asleep, but Pierre couldn't sleep slung across a galloping horse.

Every two or three hours in the rainy night Jacques had changed horses. People and horses seemed to be waiting for him. Pierre had counted six changes of horses that first night. At dawn Jacques had carried his sons in the wet sacks up to a room with a roaring fire. They had eaten and slept in the inn. After five or six hours of sleep, their journey resumed.

When they reached the swamp, Jacques had made them lie in the bottom of the boat while he rowed them about six hours to Hôtel de Jacques. Glancing at the slave notice again, Pierre was pleased their father hadn't been caught.

"I remember now," said Andrew, "Jacques wore a different cape and hat each day. He planned our escape well."

Pierre nodded, proud of their father's plan. He hoisted the chickens over a shoulder. "Put the notice in your pocket. I think we must return now."

They traveled slowly, Andrew searching for bent tree limbs he had made to mark their path. When they rested near a marsh, Pierre cut more cattail roots to eat. Opening the sack, he fed his chickens on clusters of swamp-grass seeds and let them drink. A flock of floating gray geese nodded politely as they passed. The boys splashed farther.

At sunset Andrew said, "We'll have to sleep another night in a tree. I think we've been going in circles, but now I know the way. It isn't far."

Although he felt tears in his eyes, Pierre nodded. If it wasn't far, why couldn't they keep going? He knew the answer to that. Andrew couldn't find it in darkness.

"This time we tie ourselves in the tree," he said.

"Why?" asked Andrew.

"To keep from falling. I'm tired, and so are you."

"We're not far," Andrew said. "There was a bent tree limb that led me astray."

"Here's your rope." Pierre worried about their safety. Yet he knew he couldn't complain about Andrew's getting lost, because he himself had no idea of where they were.

His twin found a comfortable branch and tied himself. When Pierre saw that his brother was safe, he tied himself, sitting on a high branch against the tree trunk.

Pierre could hardly keep his eyes open. They had reached that chicken bayou in about eight hours. Returning was taking two days. How he longed to sleep in safety.

Suddenly the booming of cannons tore through the swamp. First one after another, then several booms all at once. Ducks and geese and egrets took flight, their wings whipping the foggy night air. Nightbirds were hushed.

Andrew untied himself and climbed higher to see by the flashes of fire. "Two ships," he called, peering through the telescope. "Two ships with American flags are firing on a camp flying the British flag. The ships are the *Carolina* and the *Louisiana*." Soon he signaled that smoke had covered the light from firing cannons.

"Andrew," Pierre said, "you shouldn't have taken that ship's telescope. That belonged to the pirates."

"I know," called Andrew from high in the tree. "You should see how close it brings things!"

Pierre leaned forward across a tree limb. It was wrong for his brother to steal, but what could he do about it now? He hugged the tree branch and rested his head. Suddenly something struck his back. It settled like a coil of heavy rope, a cold coil. It moved. It shifted to fit the small of his back.

Pierre felt gooseflesh on his arms. He whistled to Andrew, and the rope behind him hissed. Pierre dared not make another sound. It seemed a snake had dropped and coiled itself against the cold December night on his warm back.

Soon the cannon fire stopped.

He heard Andrew climbing down. The moon slid from behind a shroud of gray clouds and lit the tree. Pierre hoped Andrew could see his plight.

"Don't move," Andrew whispered. "With the warmth of sunrise, the danger will pass. It's a poisonous cotton-mouth."

Pierre closed his eyes and prepared to sweat out the cold darkness. All night he dozed and woke. Whenever he moved, the snake hissed. He could imagine the waxy weave of brown, black, and white colors on the snake, the flicking tongue. A snakebite would be a slow painful death, and he wanted desperately to live to free his mother and the little sister he had never seen.

After a long night, the sun's rays shone through the trees. Warmer now, the poisonous snake uncoiled and slipped away. Pierre, drenched in dew, stared around until he found his brother. On a distant tree branch Andrew was still sleeping.

Untying himself, Pierre climbed down to the water. He gathered worms among the cypress roots at the base of the tree and fed the worms to his chickens, then let them drink the water. The hens clucked thanks and went back into the sack, but the rooster's squawks of protest wakened Andrew.

Andrew whistled greetings to his brother. Pierre whistled back, although he felt angry that Andrew hadn't cared enough to stay awake and comfort him.

But Andrew called softly, "Really, Brother, you were brave. If that had been me, I would have died of fear."

Pierre doubted that. Andrew was always brave; but it was kind of him to say it.

They continued their return and soon trees and waterways looked familiar.

"Hôtel de Jacques," Andrew said an hour later, pointing. "We made it back, Brother."

Before them stood a mighty tree, a giant of the cypress swamp. Surrounded by restless moving waters, it was thickly branched and cloaked in moss and vines.

As soon as Andrew arrived at the gnarled base of the tree trunk, he pulled himself up hand-over-hand by a vine braided around a rope. Some twenty feet above the swamp, he pushed up a trapdoor of branches still covered in bark, climbed inside, crossed himself, and bent his head.

From inside, he sent a rope down for Pierre to tie the chicken sack. As he watched Andrew hoist the chickens, free them, and drop the rope for him, Pierre wondered how long it had taken Jacques to build their hideaway.

Their tree house was like an invisible basket woven into the giant tree—Hôtel de Jacques, their father had named it. Its three stories reminded Pierre of a snug, airy birdcage.

Pierre pulled himself up on the branch floor. He closed the trapdoor to keep the chickens from falling out, then crossed himself and said a prayer of thanks. He noticed fresh bleeding as his brother used their toilet hole.

Kneeling, Pierre lowered and raised a vine-covered rope with a water cup. Water was taken upstream of their toilet opening. He poured water into a carved wooden bowl for his chickens. At the sound of pouring water, the birds stepped quickly toward the bowl and drank deeply, raising their heads to let the water slip down their feathery necks. On the return trip Pierre had gleaned a pocket full of swamp reed, rush, and wool grass seeds. He fed the chickens some of them. Then all vine-covered ropes were pulled up for the day.

The boys climbed to the second floor. "What luck! Our fire is still burning," said Andrew.

Fire smoldered in a covered iron firepot with holes in the sides near the bottom. Blowing, Andrew fed cattail straw onto the fire. When the fire was burning, Pierre set a tin pot on a tripod above it. The pot would boil water for a hot meal.

Now he could care properly for his brother's foot. Would it be infected? He unwound Andrew's bloody heel.

chapter four

As he took off the bloody stocking from Andrew's foot, Pierre said, "We must talk. If Jacques isn't coming back, what should we do?"

Fresh blood oozed around gashes on each side of his brother's heel, but Pierre saw no pus or red skin. He rinsed the wounds, and with a clean white stocking wrapped the heel again.

"I suppose we can live in the wetlands forever like swamp rats," said Andrew with a sigh. Then he looked up. "We have to explore this swamp well." He sat in front of Pierre on the branch flooring.

The second story was also woven of branches, snug and comfortable. In the corner a small brown trunk squatted mysteriously. Jacques had warned them never to open it.

Andrew pulled a big frog from a net-covered bucket and began to prepare its legs for boiling. Pierre couldn't watch. Under the net, seven other big frogs awaited their fate.

Pierre chopped cattail roots from their stored supply and to the boiling water added slices of wild onion and a red bay leaf for seasoning the frog meat. It seemed to him that Andrew relished butchering the squirming slippery frog.

Monsieur Owl, their neighbor in the giant tree, took flight in the evening air with a cry, *Who calls you?* Pierre flinched. "I don't think we can live for ourselves alone," he told Andrew. "Jacques left us to return for Isabel."

"And our baby sister," said Andrew.

The little girl would be about three years old. Their mother Isabel had been pregnant when she was sold three years before. What a horrible day!

Pierre shuddered as he remembered the marquis, with whip in hand, forcing the twins to dance jigs as their mother was driven away. She had been bound and screaming in a slaver's cart.

Andrew had refused to believe that Isabel had been sold. For months he expected her return, and whenever they stole time to be together at night, he had laughed at Pierre's worry. Pierre had danced for the marquis's guests in a lonely fog, unable to get through to his brother. He still carried the ache for his mother in his heart.

Now Isabel was being sold again, she and the little sister. Jacques had shown them the notice of sale. They had to rescue her from the slave warehouse, or buy her at auction somehow. But the warehouse was well guarded against escape or attack, and there was now a price on their heads. How could they free her?

"We may have to free them ourselves," Pierre said, "if Jacques doesn't return."

"Anyone who visited the marquis's drawing room will

recognize us," Andrew muttered. "And people of New Orleans know us because he drove the streets with us decorating each side of his carriage. I'm sure that right now kidnappers are searching for us in order to get that thousand-dollar reward."

"But that's what we may have to do," said Pierre. "We may have to buy our mother and sister."

"Or help them escape."

"I don't know which is more impossible," Pierre said. "It's three days travel time to New Orleans. How can we arrange to free them?"

Andrew stared through the woven wall.

Pierre pulled off his black velvet pantaloons. "These clothes are ridiculous," he said, and he threw them across the room. "If Jacques isn't coming back, we'll have to manage for ourselves. We better do something about our clothes."

In the corner were bolts of cloth in brown and green. "We can sew," he told his brother. "We must." He had often watched the women cut and sew, and they had both helped their mother sew for rushed occasions. Now what they had learned would help.

Squatting on the floor, Pierre measured his pants on the dark-brown wool Jacques had left them. Along with bolts of cloth, there were cutting blades, scissors, needles, and thread. Jacques had also supplied the hideaway with pots and pans, tools, coils of rope, and bread flour that had since molded.

"We must have new clothes," said Pierre, "clothes that'll hide us better. And tomorrow we break open Jacques's trunk."

It felt good to do something. Besides, he thought, I have to show Andrew that I can act, too.

He glanced over his shoulder at the small, leather-covered trunk. Light from the fire danced on its top, a domed lid sealed with rusty lock and clasps. Tomorrow they would know why Jacques had forbidden them to open it.

The next morning Pierre yawned and stretched on his bedroll. Sitting up, he wrapped his scratchy woolen blanket around him and gazed through the woven wall to view their green kingdom.

A flock of white herons with black feathered crowns flapped past. His curtains of gray-green moss trembled in the wing breeze. He heard loud rackets of feeding ducks and geese. His rooster crowed. Songbirds, frogs, and bobcats sang a swamp serenade of whistles, piping, chirps, calls, grunts, growls, and deep-voice *wahhs*.

Across the stream of flowing water below Hôtel de Jacques lay Lettuce Lake. Water lettuce carpeted the lake with emerald green velvety leaves. Pierre had thought the plants might be good food, but Andrew had said, "No animals eat the leaves, Brother. That probably means they're poisonous." Lettuce Lake was where Dagger-tooth the alligator hid, waiting for a duck to paddle by.

Three slider turtles with yellow eyes sunned on a log. A snowy egret stood there to feed on unwary frogs. A brown long-neck limpkin cried its eerie wailing call. Pierre shivered. All these swamp creatures were struggling to survive, and he and Andrew were like them.

When his chickens clucked, Pierre wondered if people

rowing by would hear those chickens and find Hôtel de Jacques. Were the two of them less safe now?

The barred owl that shared their tree flew in from its nightly hunt. Madame Owl chirped a welcome. She had already returned. Looking around him Pierre counted a dozen bright green lizards. American chameleons, the lizards changed color to brown when they rested.

Pierre thought that he and Andrew were changing colors as well. Instead of wearing white, red, and green, the brothers would now blend in with the swamp in dark brown.

From his blanket Andrew said, "Maybe Jacques is only busy."

Pierre jumped. He hadn't realized that his brother was awake. Why was it, he wondered, that Andrew never wanted to admit anything? He had waited for Isabel for months after the marquis had sold her. Now he wasn't willing to admit that Jacques was gone.

"I don't think so," Pierre said with a frown. "He would have come by now. And, at any rate, Isabel will be sold at auction January ninth."

"How do you know?" asked Andrew. He sat up and hugged his knees.

"I saw. Didn't you read the paper?" Pierre remembered the notice of sale. Jacques had tucked it behind the trunk. Yes, here it was. His hand closed on the sheet of paper.

"I didn't remember Jacques when I saw him." Andrew's voice was low and trembly.

Pierre nodded. "I didn't either," he said.

Slavery was such a strange way to live. Friends and

family being sold, new slaves being bought. They had grown up cared for by different elderly slave women like Aunt Berniece. They knew who their mother was, but times with her were stolen hours or frantic hours helping her sew.

Although they were twins, they had worked and slept far apart from each other. Their dance master had orders to keep them from talking to each other. Whistled messages took the place of talk.

Sometimes Pierre wondered what having a family, as the white masters had, would be like. He wanted a family desperately.

He stared into the huge eyes of Monsieur Owl as a mouse tail disappeared down its throat. He shivered, opened the slave auction paper, and handed it to his brother. Andrew read it in a whisper: " 'On January ninth, 1815, the Bienvieux Brothers are selling seventy-two choice slaves. Isabel Marie Alexandre, thirty-five, and daughter, three.' " Andrew rose quickly and nailed both sheets, the auction paper and the reward notice, on the wall.

Pierre stared and glanced down through the branches. "No, no, white can be seen from the water. That's not safe." He jumped up and tore the notices down.

Andrew reached over and pushed Pierre, then he kicked him and yelled, "You always stop me! Who do you think you are? My master?"

They wrestled for a few moments.

"It's awful being a twin," Andrew yelled. "I don't even own my face. You look just like me, and I hate it!"

Pierre was astonished. Was this why Andrew wouldn't

answer him sometimes? "Hush," said Pierre, pushing his brother away. He hated when his brother grew angry, but Andrew's anger seldom lasted long. They were both silent for a time.

Andrew shrugged. "How close is it to the day of Isabel's sale? What day is it now?"

After he added travel-day notches to the branch, Pierre counted from his makeshift calendar. "Are there thirty days or thirty-one in November?"

"Thirty."

"Andrew," Pierre said in a hushed voice, "I think today is December twenty-fourth. Christmas Eve."

Christmas, Easter, and the Feast of St. John the Baptist in June were three holidays the slaves were allowed to celebrate. On Christmas Eve every slave boy on Marquis De Ville's estate received a piece of hard candy and a toy: whistle, fishhook, piece of string, or marble. And the clothing allowances were made the day after Christmas. All year long, slave children looked forward to Christmas.

Pierre swallowed hard. He touched the trunk. "Here we have a surprise gift." Then he pointed to the roll of coarse brown wool, "And there we have our new clothing. If we work together, we can have new outfits for Christmas."

Andrew nodded, then whistled—danger!

Both boys quietly climbed a ladder through another trapdoor and onto the third story. This room was largest of all. From here they could see for miles, and the carefully woven roof diverted rainwater into hollow logs for use. Four doors in the curved basketlike walls led out onto sturdy cypress branches. If ever found, they could escape from here and swing to a nearby tree. Jacques had thought of everything.

As they crawled out one door now, they saw strange scenes below them. Ten or more miles away, but clearly visible by strong sunlight, they saw many longboats. British soldiers sat in scarlet red jackets and white pants, with glinting muskets in hand and knapsacks as lumps on their backs.

"The British are bringing in soldiers," Andrew whispered, staring through his telescope. To Pierre the stream of longboats looked like red ants on parade.

"They must have big ships on Lake Borgne," Pierre said. "But look over there!"

"Mud?" asked Andrew. "What is that wall?"

In the distance, far from the British line of longboats, they saw Americans in dark clothes climbing up and down like dung beetles on a muddy hill that hadn't been there three days before.

"Earthworks," said Pierre. "I heard something about that one night in the chateau drawing room. I heard that General Jackson intended to build a hill of earth to hide behind and fire on the British."

Andrew spoke louder. "I want to help them! Why can't we fight the British?"

Pierre whispered, "Hush. Remember, we're treasure for kidnappers." Pierre rested his hand on his brother's shoulder and squeezed. He wiggled to sit cross-legged on two tree limbs.

Andrew's shoulders drooped. "Why were we born slaves?"

Pierre shrugged.

"I want to be white and the only child of a wealthy master. Then I would own slaves and I could do anything I wanted."

Pierre stared at Andrew. His twin wanted to be white, like the masters who were cruel to slaves? Why would Andrew feel that way?

Andrew tore some Spanish moss loose and threw it toward the water. Pierre caught his arm in warning, and together they sat in statue stillness staring down.

Forty feet or more below them, men huddled in a boat. When had they come there? Pierre counted five men. Two black men were bareheaded; one of them had a mustache and whiskers, the other had a bushy beard. Another man had reddish hair sticking out around a yellow scarf. A fourth, a clean shaven man with mustache curled on the ends, wore all black with glints of gold and silver jewelry. A brown dog lay at his feet. The fifth man was clean shaven with shoulder-long black hair. He was neatly dressed with one blue eye staring up and one black eye patch.

Pierre saw that one man lacked a hand on one arm, another had no ears, another only one leg.

Andrew mouthed the word, "Pirates!"

chapter five

Pierre hoped the chickens wouldn't reveal the hideaway to the pirates below. That morning in the dark the rooster had crowed for an hour. Now he could hear the chickens clucking and walking about. Why had Andrew wanted that hen?

Aunt Berniece had told Pierre that he was the wise one, that he should take care of Andrew. He should have known better than to let Andrew take chickens that might give them away.

Of course, he thought, neither he nor Andrew had known that the swamp would suddenly come alive with British and American armies and navies, and people building earthworks.

Pierre nodded ever so slowly to Andrew. Yes, these were pirates all right. Everyone in New Orleans whispered about the cruel pirate captain, Jean Lafitte. The pirates had a sea fortress on a beautiful Gulf of Mexico island called Grand Terre.

With a start, Pierre realized that if they had a clear view down, the pirates had the same view up. He motioned to Andrew to begin crawling back into Hôtel de Jacques. Chips of bark scattered. The floor creaked. Disturbed,

Monsieur and Madame Owl blinked their large green eyes. Monsieur hooted twice, but being used to their boy neighbors, the owls soon tucked their heads under their wings and returned to sleep.

At the owl's hoot, a pirate below them yelled and began to row clear of the giant cypress tree. "I tell you numskulls, it's bad magic," he called.

"Steady now, you chuckle-headed fool. What can an owl do to us?" That was the blue-eyed pirate with the eye patch.

"Bad magic, I say. Don't you know that? Red-eye always said an owl's hoot in daylight meant a traitor was near."

"Red-eye is dead."

"That's what I mean." In the silence that followed, the pirates looked from one to another.

"Where's Black Jack? He has tarried over long." The eye-patch pirate seemed to be the one who asked that. "Black Jack was never a chuckle-headed numskull." Even from that distance the eye-patch pirate looked like someone Pierre had seen before.

"Truly," asked one of the black pirates, "where does Black Jack sleep tonight?" Leaning, he looked into the waters and laughed. Pierre felt a tingle along his spine.

Two of the pirates chuckled. "Now we have his share of the gold!" One of them slapped the boat as he laughed.

The pirates were so involved in conversation that Andrew dropped from third story to first to stare at them. Pierre followed more slowly, allowing the creaking ladder to blend with frog calls and birdsong. The chickens ran to him clucking, and he filled their grain bowl to quiet them. After the chickens began eating, Pierre lay on his stomach beside Andrew, who was staring at the pirates through floor spaces.

Suddenly Pierre stood and climbed the ladder to bring down the brown wool from the second floor. He spread out the cloth for him and Andrew to lie on. He had realized that their white underwear might be visible through spaces in the floor.

"Back under the tree, you sniveling puppies," ordered the black-haired pirate. "I will not have them see us first."

"Aye, aye, Captain." Now the boat returned to float under Hôtel de Jacques.

Andrew smiled at Pierre. Pierre wondered if his brother had gone crazy. Murderous pirates sat below them in a boat. The hens had snuggled up to his side and might squawk. The rooster might crow. At any moment they might be discovered. What was there for Andrew to smile about?

He knew the answer: Andrew had plans. His brother's plans were usually some kind of mischief, but sometimes his plans were good.

It was Andrew who had known enough to keep a supply of cattail roots to eat; Andrew knew about seasoning with wild onions and red bay leaf and serving wild garlic bulbs with boiled fish or frog legs. Andrew fished, hunted, and harvested. He tied rope in trees and provided a way to travel. An Indian boy who worked for the marquis had taught Andrew how to survive in a swampland. Pierre had never spoken to that boy.

The problem was, Andrew made only quick day-to-day plans, while Pierre knew they needed more: They needed to work out a way to free Isabel and their little sister. Impossible maybe. But then, maybe not!

He smiled back at Andrew. Somehow he felt sure that together he and Andrew could unite their family.

A hen stalked away from Pierre. He dared not grab it.

"Captain Lafitte," called the frightened pirate. "Put off from this tree. I smell chicken blood and death." The pirate lowered his voice. "We all know ghosts visited camp three days ago. I say we finish our ship repairs and sail away from Mr. Madison's War with the British."

The other pirates chuckled nervously. Captain Lafitte gazed up sniffing. Mouth open, heart drumming, Pierre watched his hen squat and poop through the floor directly into the pirate captain's face.

Lafitte roared, bolted upright, and almost fell out of the boat. He cursed with flailing arms. The pirates rowed until they were under another tree several yards away. Choked in silent laughter, Pierre and Andrew rolled on their backs.

Captain Lafitte's face was red, his ears were flaming. "You're all sniveling puppies!" he yelled.

Now Pierre and Andrew could watch through the wall. The pirates continued arguing over bad magic, owls' hoots in daytime, and fox fire steps across the island. Unnoticed, out of the swirling silvery mist a longboat slid toward them. Two redcoat soldiers and two officers with gold braid on red coats stared at the pirates.

"Ahoy, Captain," called a British officer.

"Ahoy," said Jean Lafitte.

"Captain Jean Lafitte, I presume?"

"You presume rightly."

"I am a lieutenant of His Majesty's Royal Army."

Jean Lafitte folded his arms.

"I have been given orders to seek your aid in the war against the American states," the officer said.

The pirates exchanged quick glances. Uncrossing his arms, Lafitte sat, hands on knees, and stared at the British officer.

"Aye, sir," he said, "and what is in it for us?"

"I have been given orders to offer thirty thousand pounds, and to Captain Jean Lafitte, sir, a captaincy in His Majesty's navy."

Pierre nodded to Andrew. The deep hoarse voice was the same. This was the lieutenant whose boat had sailed under the slave notice. That day he hadn't called the pirates "sir"! Pierre raised his eyebrows at Andrew.

"Thirty thousand pounds apiece?" asked the pirate chief.

The lieutenant seemed startled. "Thirty thousand to be shared among you . . . pirates. Among your . . . Gulf Coast Brotherhood."

"And," asked Lafitte, "are all my men offered captaincies on ships in His Majesty's navy?" While his voice was loud and demanding, his fingers played with the puppy's fur.

Pierre raised his eyebrows again. Jean Lafitte was tricky.

"No, sir. Only you, Captain Lafitte, but the others may be hired on our ships. I will confer with General

Parkenham, sir. He is bringing up reinforcements, four thousand strong by Christmas Day, sir."

Pierre stared at Andrew.

"Sir," the lieutenant went on, rubbing his neck, "we had a surprise attack. Two ships showered us with grapeshot and round shot, sir. Our reinforcements are arriving, sir, and we intend to attack New Orleans. But we need your scouting. We need to avoid sneak attacks in this foggy swampland."

"Which two ships?" asked Jean Lafitte. When he moved, his bracelets of gold flashed. High above the water Pierre heard his jewelry clink.

"The ships were the fourteen-gun *Carolina*, and twenty-two-gun *Louisiana*, sir."

Andrew had watched that battle, and Pierre had slept with a poisonous snake that night. Pierre shivered and wondered if, when the British, the pirates, and the Americans were busy fighting a war, he and Andrew could sneak past them and free Isabel and their sister. Maybe no one would be looking for runaway slave boys!

He knew it wasn't true. The marquis had offered a big reward for them.

"Lieutenant," said Jean Lafitte in a voice suddenly like pancake syrup, "we will consider your offer. Tell your general that last September the Americans fired on our sea fortress on Grand Terre Island. We pirates are thirsty for revenge!"

"Thank you, sir," said the lieutenant, smiling. "Thank you." He reached to shake hands with Lafitte, but the pirate folded his arms. Saluting, the redcoat lowered his hand.

"In that attack," he said, "we lost many men in the dark. Those Americans do not fight honestly in noble battles face-to-face. General Keane seeks safety from such surprise attacks."

"We will contact you with the place and time for our next meeting," Lafitte said.

The redcoats backed their boat, turned, and began to row away. Raising an arm, the lieutenant stopped the longboat. "Sir," he said, "I was to tell you." Glancing around in the swirling mists, he lowered his voice. "Sir, our password is 'Beauty and booty.' In case you approach our camp or our boats. 'Beauty and booty.'"

Lafitte simply stared at him.

The redcoat saluted again.

Pierre's rooster stood. It preened its feathers and strutted about the room. Then it crowed, and crowed, and crowed.

chapter six

The pirate with black eye patch called, "Ho, brothers, methinks we pirates should find that swamp rooster." As he stared over his shoulder toward Hôtel de Jacques, he smiled. Pierre felt it was a wicked smile, and he held his breath.

However, the frightened bushy-haired pirate and his friend rowed the boat away, leaping across the water. They rowed so rapidly they passed the British in their longboat. "Bad magic," Pierre heard the pirates muttering.

Soon their green kingdom returned to its usual medley of animal sounds, and the mirrorlike waters smelled clean. The boats had stirred red and yellow leaves deep in the water, but now the leaves were shifting back and forth peacefully.

When the boats were far away, Pierre turned to his brother. "Andrew, we have to return these chickens. Just now, they almost gave us away!"

"No, no," said Andrew, "we need those delicious eggs. You never like my ideas." He frowned.

"We're in danger here," said Pierre with arms outstretched. "Remember, we have to free Isabel and our sister. We can't get caught because of chicken eggs." He pushed Andrew's arm.

Andrew pushed him back and grabbed his elbow.

Pierre jerked free. "We've eaten for six weeks without those chickens."

"But, Pierre, you like hens. You used to clean up after the marquis's chickens. Old Hen Heart." Andrew patted Pierre's shoulder. "We have to open Jacques's trunk, remember? And sew some clothes. I'm cold."

Yes, they needed to cut and sew before they could do anything else. Pierre knew that. Andrew was right, but suppose the pirates returned looking for the rooster?

At noon he was busy cutting cloth, and Andrew searched for tools to open the trunk. For lunch they ate cattail roots and wild onion shoots.

"Let the trunk be," Pierre said. "We need our clothes finished." Andrew agreed, and sewing took up all the rest of the day. They stitched the seams well. The suits would be sturdy.

As his brother sewed, Pierre made him soak his foot. The cuts still showed no red streaks. Pierre had washed and dried white silk stockings for clean bandages.

That evening Andrew said, "Help me pull the trunk into the center."

Pierre stood on the other side. Together they shoved the heavy trunk in little movements. Inside something rattled noisily with each move. Pierre stared out between branches of Hôtel de Jacques. No one seemed near to hear the rattle. Only Monsieur and Madame Owl noticed. Blinking kindly, they stared at their young neighbors.

With the last shove, something inside the trunk fell against metal. The brothers stared at each other. Andrew tried pounding a hammer on the rusty lock. "My guess is the trunk holds tools."

"I don't think that hammering noise is wise," Pierre said. He returned to sewing.

"You know," said his brother as he tried to pry the lid with a stick, "we shouldn't tell anyone our names." The stick broke.

"Who's asking?"

"No one yet."

"All right."

"We can take new names," Andrew said.

Pierre glanced up. "Gator Bait and Hen Heart?"

Andrew looked surprised. "Sure, if someone hears Gator Bait or Hen Heart they won't think we're Andrew or Pierre Alexandre."

"We could shorten the last name to Alex. Hen Heart Alex, Gator Bait Alex."

"No," said Andrew, "we don't need a last name. Besides, did you hear those pirates? The man with the black eye patch was called Evil Eye Alex."

Pierre shuddered. "That rooster almost gave us away. As soon as we finish these clothes, Gator Bait, we return the chickens." He decided to insist on it.

Andrew shrugged.

By midnight, Pierre had two jackets and trousers together, but his brother was still fighting the trunk.

"Gator Bait," he said, "you turn hems." When he had threaded a needle for Andrew, he said, "Forget that trunk for a while. We can't waste time trying to open it."

Pierre felt angry. He slapped the trunk twice, once on Andrew's side and once on his own. Then he leaned on the trunk to reach for a jacket to stitch.

The rusty lock popped open. As if hands inside were lifting it, the lid raised slowly. The brothers stared at the trunk, stared at each other. The lock that had appeared rusty was shiny clean and well-oiled inside.

Black cloth lay across whatever else was in the trunk. Andrew started to reach inside, but Pierre caught his hand.

"No, no," he whispered. "I've heard that sometimes these trunks have traps."

He picked up a fish knife. Andrew leaned back. Pierre touched the black cloth, and a dagger sprang past his fish knife. It flew to the ceiling with a loud twang and stuck in a tree branch.

Pierre stared. No wonder Jacques had told them never to open the trunk. If his brother hadn't leaned back, that dagger would have been in his heart. The boys stared at each other. Pierre crossed himself.

Tapping the black cloth released three other daggers. Two hit the ceiling and fell. One passed out the wall and splashed in the swamp waters below.

Andrew handed Pierre the hammer claw. Crouched on the floor, Pierre used the claw to jerk the black cloth off. A sword swung from right to left across the trunk with a soft swish. The slicing sword had been wired under the folded cloth. It might have slit a throat!

When his pounding heart had almost returned to normal, Pierre peeked into the trunk and saw a folded paper. Using two sticks, he lifted the note from the trunk and gave it to Andrew who opened it, but they saw nothing.

"Why?" asked Pierre in a whisper. "Why would Jacques have a note with nothing written on it?"

"Wait," Andrew said. "Haven't you heard about invisible ink? Maybe it's a note written in ink that needs something to let one see it."

"Well," said Pierre, "how do you make it visible?"

His brother frowned. "Sometimes juice of a lemon or apple vinegar works. Or sometimes heat brings out the writing." He stared around. "Or maybe this steam will work?"

The water pot sat over their fire. He held the note over the steaming water. Words came to view.

SEA CHEST OF BLACK JACK
PIRATE OF THE GULF BROTHERHOOD

The signature of Jacques Alexandre was at the bottom. Pierre could not believe it. Their father a pirate? What a thing to learn on Christmas Eve night!

When Andrew moved the parchment paper away from the steam, the words faded. His hand trembled.

"We're sons of a pirate," whispered Pierre. He covered his face. "God help us!"

Andrew snapped his fingers. "That means we should get his share of that gold. That's our money. I wish I'd taken some from that trunk when we were at the pirate camp. Now we can buy Isabel."

"How can you think about gold?" cried Pierre, waving his arms. "We're sons of a pirate! We're not just escaping slavery, we're escaping pirates, laws of Louisiana, and the Congress of Washington City!"

"It's easier to think about that chest of gold," said

Andrew. "What can we do about Louisiana or Washington City? That pirate said they would split up Black Jack's share. Well, it's ours, and I want it. We're Jacques's sons."

"Andrew," whispered Pierre, "our father was or is a pirate!"

"We hardly knew him." Andrew shrugged. "Aunt Berniece sent us out to him. He hasn't made you into a pirate, Hen Heart, nor me. What did he mean to us?" Andrew grinned. "I want his gold!"

Pierre hoped the idea of being a pirate's son didn't sound good to Andrew. The governor hung pirates and their accomplices.

Andrew peeked into the trunk. "Is it safe now?"

"Lean back." Pierre pulled the sword out. It was clean and well-oiled like the daggers. A simple notch had held its tip, and a spring had been set at the handle. Using the sword tip to lift material out and leaning away from the trunk, he removed a man's cloak and several outfits of clothing in dark merchant-style. He tossed them across the room, then peered inside.

At the bottom lay a deep layer of jewelry shining softly in the firelight. He saw strings of pearls, red rubies, sparkling diamonds, gem-encrusted bracelets and necklaces, green emerald brooches.

"Enough to buy Isabel and the little sister!" Andrew called. Laughing, he reached into the trunk. "What a Christmas Eve gift!"

As his hands touched the jewels, an explosion knocked them both to the floor. Their owl neighbors screeched and flew away.

chapter seven

The last trap had been a flintlock pistol, loaded and ready. Pierre saw a string under the jewelry that might have triggered it to fire. His brother lay face down on the black cloth cover, but Pierre saw no blood.

"Pierre," said Andrew in muffled voice, "we should run. Not only have they heard the rooster, but now the loud shot. The pirates and the British will come to see what happened. Those chickens might give us away. And what about Jacques's jewels? Let's cover the trunk and run."

"Yes," Pierre said. "You're right." At last Andrew agreed that the chickens weren't safe to have around.

He sighed. "It's cold, but we'll take those chickens. Maybe going will keep Hôtel de Jacques from being discovered."

"Now we have our new clothes," said Andrew, rising to hands and knees. He was wearing his new attire.

Pierre looked at his brother's outfit and felt proud of himself. The long trousers had been the hardest part, but they bent in the seat, buttoned at the waist, and were loose for swinging in the swamps.

The jacket buttoned to the neck, with full-length sleeves and comfortable shoulder space. Everything had hemmed edges and whipped buttonholes to avoid tearing. Best of all, the outfits were warm. He had to admit that he and Andrew had done a great job of sewing. Isabel would be pleased with their work tonight.

Soon they would be out in the cold of a December night. Maybe he should have made hoods to sew on the jackets!

"And we can tie these leather bags on our feet."

"What leather bags?" Pierre asked.

Andrew pointed in the trunk.

Pierre slid over and felt them. "They have a draw-string, Gator Bait. I saw the marquis with money in bags like these. These are Jacques's money bags!"

Andrew sat to pull on his new shoes. "They fit snug as a wedding band," he said. "Maybe they'll bring us good luck!"

Pierre closed the sea chest. He opened the black cloth to throw over it. "Andrew," he called, "look!"

The cloth was a sack that held two flags, one red and one black. On both sides of the black flag someone had sewn a white skull over a white hourglass at the center, and under these a white sword the length of the flag. The same three emblems were sewn on both sides of the red flag.

Pierre threw the flags aside, then tossed the men's clothing over the trunk to hide it. As he climbed down to stuff the sleepy chickens into their sack, he said, "We'll throw those pirate flags in the swamp."

"No," said Andrew. "Those pirate flags may save our lives. One day we might have to bargain with them. Who knows? We'll take the chickens and sleep in a tree somewhere near here."

"Let's hurry," said Pierre.

Within minutes they prepared bags of cattail roots to carry. With the sack of chickens over his shoulder, Pierre dropped down to the cypress roots, then swung out and Andrew followed. Pierre had never swung out first before. When he glanced over his shoulder, he saw surprise on his brother's face.

Across the water they climbed another tree. They had traveled for half an hour when Andrew whistled and pointed.

By moonlight Pierre saw an overturned boat floating toward them. Some fisherman or soldier must have lost it. Maybe it had something to do with the people fighting the war. Andrew dropped slowly on the rope and waited for the small boat, sharply pointed at each end, to drift by. Swamp people called these boats *pirogues*. Wouldn't a boat be wonderful! thought Pierre. Was this a floating Christmas gift?

Snagging it, Andrew flipped it over and dropped inside. He stood carefully, still holding the rope. Pierre could see no water pouring in. Wonderful! Now they could travel faster and safely.

Since they had no oars, the twins used daggers to cut off two long branches and trim the twigs. These made sturdy poles to push their way through the swamp. The poles were long enough to reach the bottom of the swamp in most places.

Silently they pushed their pirogue through the waters. When they reached a stretch of marsh grass, they stopped. They were now far enough away.

"Look," Pierre said, "we can hide the boat in this marsh. I'll tie bunches of grass around the sides."

In the safety of their boat, they slept well all night.

The next morning Andrew said, "We look like an invisible island. We're really hidden by this grass you tied around the boat. Hen Heart, you're a clever rascal."

Pierre winced. "I'm not a rascal, just a boy."

His brother nodded. "Sons of a pirate, what a surprise! But that doesn't mean we have to be robbers. I've decided I want to be a rich merchant when I grow up."

If we live to grow up, Pierre thought. "When did you decide?"

"Those pirate flags made me think. I don't want to drift like seaweed and end up like Jacques. I need a plan."

Pierre nodded. It was pleasant talking as friends, as brothers. "I think I'd like to be a farmer. But first we must free Isabel, then we have to buy ourselves free."

"Truth is," said Andrew, "we may have to live like swamp rats all our lives, even if we buy our mother and sister. But we're closer to buying them. We have Jacques's gems."

"Let's return these chickens fast," Pierre said in a whisper. "They put us in danger."

By a clear morning sky they poled the boat to the chicken bayou in a little more than four hours. When Pierre released the chickens, they seemed to recognize their home. The rooster ran squawking, and the hens ran in jerky chicken steps behind it. Andrew poled the boat to hide in marsh grass near the bayou.

"Grandpapa," called a little girl's voice. "Picayune is back with his hens."

Pierre watched the hens. When I'm a farmer, he

thought, I'll have many warm-bodied chickens and I'll make them all my pets. He was pleased that his chickens had a family to care for them. And he sighed in relief that he was no longer a thief.

When he heard squishy footsteps, he slid down in the boat and pulled Andrew after him. A white-haired man who was short with bow legs had come to the child's call. He stood staring across the bayou.

As the man turned to follow the little girl, Andrew asked in a whisper, "Does he look kindly?"

"Why?"

"Maybe we could get him to buy Isabel for us."

Pierre wondered: Could they trust the man? The poor Cajun might take the jewels and use them for himself.

Andrew said, "Maybe we won't give him Black Jack's pirate jewels, but as his sons we're due his share of the pirate gold. We'll use gold to buy Isabel and the little sister. Everyone accepts gold."

"What gold?" asked Pierre. "Are you thinking about stealing from pirates? We escaped once. Let's not push our luck."

Andrew kicked him. "You, Hen Heart! You never want to do anything rally rousing. You would still be sitting in Hôtel de Jacques starving if I hadn't fished for you. You can't even kill a frog! Come on."

What Andrew said was true. But was it right to steal gold from pirates, even if it might be yours?

"You agree that we need gold," Andrew said, sitting up and putting his pole in the water. "Let's go. From our boat we can spy on the pirates. We know where their island is, we know everything about the place. And maybe they won't be there."

Pierre peeked over the grasses. The little girl and her grandfather seemed to have gone. It was peaceful, and there was something he needed to say.

"Andrew," he said softly, "Merry Christmas!"

"Christmas?" asked his brother. "What a Christmas!"

Pierre saw tears in Andrew's eyes. They had slept Christmas Eve night in a pirogue deep in a dangerous swamp. All alone. Slavery had been more secure than this.

No. He mustn't feel that slavery had been good, and he mustn't let Andrew think that either. He suspected his brother was thinking of past Christmases.

"Remember the mean parts of living with the marquis," Pierre said. "How he forced us to dance for his guests. How the servants wouldn't feed us properly because of his orders. Remember that he sold Isabel away from us."

Andrew nodded. "I would rather die free than live as a slave, but every night I think of my soft bed, of reading and ciphering classes, of Aunt Berniece and Aunt Marie and Aunt Joanna who loved us."

They sat in silence. Birds seemed to sing Christmas carols, and in the distance a flock of honking geese took flight, their wings flapping noisily.

Andrew began pushing their boat toward the pirates' island. Pierre lowered his pole and sighed. With the boat they could be there in about an hour. But should they go?

chapter eight

As they poled closer to the pirates, Pierre heard singing. The voices were deep, and the song more grunted than sung. He put a hand on Andrew to stop him, but Andrew poled toward the sea of grass across from the pirates' island. They swished into the middle of the tall rushes under a glaring sun. Pierre listened to the pirates' song:

"Fearless strong and pirate bold,
It's gold doubloons and pieces of eight.
Bars of silver, bars of gold,
T'was gold dinars what sealed our fate.
Fearless strong and pirate bold. . . ."

Pierre shivered and lay low in the pirogue. He felt naked in the open sunlight. If a pirate climbed a tree, he could look down on them. Pierre could only hope they were safe.

Slowly his brother poled their boat farther across the high marsh grass. Now looking between tree trunks Pierre could see the pirates. Four were playing cards; three were polishing guns and singing; and seven sat talking. Several pirates were of African ancestry. Three brown puppies scampered among the pirates. Now and then one pirate or another reached out to catch a puppy and scratch behind its ears.

Through verses of the song, Pierre could hear bits of conversation:

"Lafitte's no hen-hearted fool," said a voice.

Pierre cringed, and Andrew grinned at him. Pierre kicked at his brother and stuck out his tongue. Andrew shoved Pierre's foot away. They began scuffling, but stopped to overhear the pirates.

"More money from . . . American scoundrels with Jackson?"

"No money. Something for all . . . crafty brotherhood."

"Besides, sniveling chuckle-headed British . . . emptied treasury fighting Napoleon. Numskull Americans . . . free brotherhood . . . laws of piracy."

"Pardon for all? . . . all?"

What? thought Pierre. Captain Lafitte was going to aid the Americans rather than the British? And for a pardon? Pirates were outlaws of the worse kind. Whenever a pirate was caught, he was hanged.

"Fear not," said another pirate voice. "Lafitte . . . no fool. Pardoned pirates . . . own the world!"

Was it fair to pardon these murderers? Wars made people do strange things. Pierre shook his head.

Two pirates smoking pipes walked down by the water. The men were only four or five pole lengths away.

Andrew seemed so relaxed. Didn't he see that the men might glance over and see their boat? The grass tied around their pirogue was a different color green from the rushes they were in.

Pierre watched Andrew's hand slide off the side of the boat and onto a plant. He pulled it back slowly and handed

Pierre a snail. Pierre sucked the snail free from its shell. How cool, juicy, and chewy it was. Joining Andrew, Pierre began plucking snails off grass ever so slowly. Snails were a French treat the marquis seldom allowed.

The smoking pirates walked away, and by midafternoon most of the other pirates had fallen asleep. They simply stretched out and began snoring. One thing was clear— none of them seemed bothered by the gunshot last night. Hôtel de Jacques seemed safe.

When Pierre had accounted for all the pirates, he nodded for his brother to begin poling out of the tall rushes. Pierre had quietly replaced the grasses around their pirogue so that they blended in.

The sound of swishing through the grass was so noisy, however, that a flock of gray geese flew off with loud honking. Andrew stopped poling and looked at Pierre. They couldn't move. They were trapped until night.

While they lay warm in the sun, Pierre tried to plan. Andrew was right. If they could find someone trustworthy, they could send that person to buy Isabel and their sister free. Jacques's jewels would possibly pay for their freedom.

But where would they find someone trustworthy? He didn't trust the Cajun who owned the chickens. Something about the way the man stood worried him. Besides, he had probably read one of the notices offering a reward for them.

Wait. Pierre blinked. That man *was* the person who had nailed the runaway notices to the trees. He remembered the round body and bow legs. That was why he had seemed familiar. Of course. The marquis paid someone who lived in the swamp to nail reward notices there.

Pierre planned to tell Andrew when they could talk. His brother mustn't trust that Cajun fisherman.

Well, where could they find someone?

How about the Americans building General Jackson's earthworks? Pierre remembered hearing that General Jackson had sent for riflemen from as far as Kentucky and Tennessee. Would an American come to their aid?

Not all Americans approved of owning slaves. Some, he had heard, helped slaves to get free. Others wanted new states joining the union to be free of slavery. How could they find someone like that? It seemed impossible, but maybe it wasn't.

He must take courage and hope for the best. He had hoped for his brother's foot to heal, and it was better. With that thought, Pierre fell asleep.

It was dark when he awoke. Andrew's head lay on his legs and his toes were bent under with cramps. Pierre raised his head to peek around. The island had three yellow fires crackling in the dark. The light showed pirates passing rum bottles filled at a keg and passing meat cooked on bayonets stuck into the fire. The roasted meat smelled delicious.

He covered Andrew's lips as he jiggled him awake. His brother gasped, but made no other sound as he woke up. Sitting up in the boat, Pierre rubbed his cramped toes and tingling legs. He pointed to the poles.

Each of them had taken a pole and begun pushing, when they heard a shout: "Ho, mates!"

"Ho," answered pirates on the island.

A man in a longboat called, "We finished scraping the

ship today. You numskulls begin caulking and tarring tomorrow."

The twins backed their pirogue into the sea of grass again. It seemed they couldn't leave yet. From the boats they heard the man's song:

"Earn ye bottle of rum, pirate bold,
Sight ship, board her, find her gold."

On shore the pirates sang:

"Dum dee dum, ho!
Earn our rum, ho!
Dum dee dum, ho!
Share all 'n one, ho!"

The pirate on the boat had a strong tenor voice. He sang the next verse:

"We rob the wealth of those rich and high,
Not poor folk commoners such as I."

From the shore came:

"Dum dee dum, ho!
Earn our rum, ho!
Dum dee dum, ho!
Share all 'n one, ho!"

The singing was so noisy that as soon as the new pirates pulled up by the island Andrew swished out. Together they began pushing the pirogue away. Pierre thought they must look like a drifting clump of grass.

When he raised his head to glance back, he saw the eye-patch pirate named Evil Eye Alex staring after them. Arms folded, he leaned against an oak and watched them glide away.

Pierre tapped Andrew to look, but his brother was sliding around a fallen tree and heading for Hôtel de Jacques. Pierre whistled danger, but Andrew didn't look back. Pierre frowned.

Exploring the swamp had paid off. Andrew had a better sense of direction now, and even Pierre recognized the way. Sitting up, they both pushed their pirogue by the light from the moon. In three hours they were back at Hôtel de Jacques. No one had bothered it.

In spite of his afternoon nap, Pierre slept soundly that Christmas night.

The next morning when Pierre awoke and sat up to enjoy gazing over their green kingdom, he smiled. He could hardly wait to tell Andrew about his idea of visiting the earthworks to find an American friend. If his rooster and hens had been there, they would have crowed by then and cackled for food. He missed petting them.

Andrew awoke with a start. "We must pack things in our boat," he said. "I think we have a busy day ahead."

Pierre sighed and wondered what new danger they would find now.

chapter nine

Pierre convinced Andrew that they should breakfast together. They said grace and ate wild onions and cattails. Afterward Andrew began cutting rope in lengths. Jacques had left them coils and coils of sturdy brown rope, the kind that was used as ship's line.

On one rope Andrew attached the black pirate flag. "The Jolly Roger," he said. He seemed to be plotting some new scheme. With a sigh Pierre decided not to ask what his brother was planning. Sometimes it was better not to know.

He gazed around. Taking the brown wool cloth, he cut a shallow hood. It covered his head nicely. He glanced at his brother who was busy attaching the second flag about two arm-lengths above the first. Andrew's eyes were intent on his work, but when he looked up they were gray ghost eyes.

Quickly Pierre cut hoods deep enough to fall over their faces and hide their eyes. As he sewed the hoods onto their jackets, he watched Andrew.

"What're you doing?" he asked finally.

"Flags," Andrew held them up, "on rope. Pail," he held up a pot, "for snails."

"That's good," Pierre said. He approved of going for

supplies, but what did Andrew want with those pirate flags?

Andrew pulled out a small, loosely woven sack they used for collecting. "For cattails." He began climbing down, swinging over to the pirogue, and packing it. He added a cup for water.

Pierre passed down their remaining three old shoes. Made in France, they were of soft leather and topped with large buckles of pure hammered silver. Andrew raised his eyebrows.

"If we throw these off somewhere and they're found, perhaps the marquis will think we drowned and stop looking for us," said Pierre. "Then we're Gator Bait and Hen Heart forever."

"Good," Andrew said. He swung the shoes over to the boat.

Pierre moved down, tied up their trapdoor, and draped Spanish moss to hide the rope. Usually Andrew did these things, and he watched Pierre with raised eyebrows.

"Pierre," asked Andrew, "which way to New Orleans?"

Pierre looked around. Their bald cypress was an eerie silver in morning mist, lit by the sun. That must be east, so with his left hand he pointed west.

"Good," said Andrew. "Where's the Gulf of Mexico?"

New Orleans was north of the Gulf, so the Gulf waters must be due south. Pierre pointed.

"Pirate Island is where?"

They had gone around fallen trees, marshlands of green grass, and watery stands of cypress and their knees. This wasn't fair. Pierre forced himself to remember the general direction. He pointed northeast.

Andrew flashed a smile. "Good, Hen Heart!"

Andrew shoved the pirogue out. "I want to find a steeple I saw," he said. "Someone there might help us. Mark our path."

This time Pierre paid attention to all the bent limbs and notched tree trunks. When they went beyond the path Andrew had marked earlier, he began chipping cypress knees and standing to swing branches down and snap them. This time Pierre kept orienting himself. With every turn and bend, he concentrated on his directions.

Every time they saw the runaway slave notice on a tree, one of them tore it off. There were so many the marquis must really believe they were in the wetlands. How many people knew about them? Pierre wondered.

He jerked his hood forward, and so did Andrew. A pocket or two in his jacket would have been good to hold those paper notices, he decided.

After a number of hours they slid into rushes and picked snails. Pierre pailed one, ate one. The sun was high above them, and it was good to relax in its warmth.

"Andrew," he asked, "do you think we could find an American to help us? We could visit General Jackson's earthworks and see if some rifleman would take pity on us."

Andrew nodded. "To go buy Isabel and our sister?"

"Let's give her a name. I hate calling her sister, baby sister, or little girl."

"Bella," Andrew said, as if he had already planned it. "Isabel and Bella."

"Good. I wonder what her name really is?" When their

pail was full and their stomachs full as well, they peered around carefully and swished out of the rushes.

"A rifleman might help us," Andrew said, "and he might not."

"That Cajun grandpapa was the same man who nailed the reward notices to the trees," said Pierre. He was pleased to see his brother's surprise. For a change he knew something before Andrew, and that made him feel good.

"Some people are greedy," said Andrew with a shrug. "The Cajun might help us for money."

"Greedy people will do anything if they think there's money in it," Pierre said, "but they're also cutthroats. If we went to him, he could have that reward money for capturing us, and the jewels as well."

Andrew nodded sadly. Pierre suspected his news had disappointed his brother. It was sad that they couldn't talk to each other more. Pierre wondered if the marquis had built a permanent wall between them.

Midafternoon as they cut cattail roots into chunks, the sky grew dark. December was always the dark, chilly month of the year, but this afternoon a storm seemed to be brewing.

Still Andrew poled north. After half an hour he stood. "There," he said softly, "do you see that church? I knew it was there from the steeple. Think we could get help there?"

Pierre stood as their boat slid toward a foggy tree-lined bank. They seemed to be on a stream that led to the river because they poled against the flow. Beyond a small graveyard milky with mist stood a graceful, gray stone church. The rectory for the priest was in the rear.

The riverbank was at head level, and they were peering at the church and rectory so intently, they missed seeing the alligator. The muddy green animal was at the land's edge. It opened its mouth, and white teeth flashed at Pierre. He whistled, danger! With his pole he shoved the boat away from the riverbank.

The alligator slid forward. It splashed into the water between the boat and the riverbank. Grabbing a live oak branch, Andrew swung up and leaped for land. Pierre stayed with the boat. He was frightened, but he knew they needed that boat. He wasn't about to be trapped away from Hôtel de Jacques!

He beat the alligator with his pole. He whacked it over and over across its broad green snout. As the boat slid downriver, the gator tilted the boat with webbed claws. It opened its mouth. Pierre shoved a shoe into the animal's throat and jammed it down with his pole. The animal dropped into the river.

In silence, Pierre continued whacking the snout. The gator scratched the side of the boat. Pierre grabbed one of Jacques's daggers that they had brought and chipped at the thick skin between the claws, so thick no knife could penetrate it. However, his attack made the alligator sink in the water. After taking more pounding on its thick, dirty green hide, the alligator slid under the boat and swam off.

Pierre watched in amazement. The animal must have been fifteen feet long, a grandpapa of the river. It swam deeper and disappeared in the dark water.

Andrew whistled from the riverbank. He had followed the boat down the waters. He grinned and shook his head from side to side. "*Sacré bleu!* You fought an alligator and won. I would never have done that."

"I wasn't about to lose our pirogue." Had he really fought an alligator? Pierre wondered. The thought made him feel weak.

"That was brave, Hen Heart," said Andrew. "Really brave."

Throwing Andrew a rope to tie the boat, Pierre scrambled onto the riverbank. Although he appeared casual, he was smiling to himself. Yes, he had been courageous.

They found an overhang where, hidden from land, the boat could be tied to tree roots. Andrew tied it fore and aft like a swinging cradle. "In case of a storm," he said.

Already it was late afternoon. "It's dry here," said Pierre. "Maybe we could sleep in this pit." Two trees guarded what seemed to be a hole.

He knelt and touched dry earth that formed a cavern. Patting the opening, he crept forward. Toward the back the space descended at a steep angle. It smelled of animal droppings. Air flowed over his face. Was it coming from the tree roots?

He moved cautiously forward and suddenly slipped and fell headfirst. As he dropped, he heard his brother calling.

"Pierre? Where are you, Hen Heart?"

His brother's voice grew faint, farther and farther away. Pierre grabbed all around him for support, but he kept falling.

chapter ten

Pierre woke up in the dark repeating, "Take courage, take courage, take courage." He felt a painful lump on his forehead. It must have been from a blow that had knocked him out. He sat up and rubbed his hands over his arms and legs. Other than his lump, and the ache in his head, he seemed all right.

When his eyes had adjusted, he saw a glow to his right. He tried standing, but hit his head. The roof of the cave was low.

On hands and knees he crawled toward the light. It was an uphill crawl through sharp stones and rubble that cut at his knees and hands. Wings brushed his hood as a bat flew out.

At the point of faint light, Pierre heard a whistle.

He answered with a whistle.

"Pierre, is that you?"

Who else? thought Pierre. "It's deep. Get rope," he called. His voice echoed over and over.

Pierre could hear Andrew run for rope. In minutes he returned. "I'll tie an end to this oak," said Andrew. Next Pierre heard him sliding down, pushing out from the wall as he slid.

"Welcome," said Pierre, steadying him as he reached bottom.

"This is over twenty feet deep," his brother said with a gasp. "How did you make it?" His voice trembled.

"Well, I didn't plan to fall," said Pierre. "Do you still have the rope?"

"It doesn't touch bottom."

"But we can reach it?"

"We can reach it."

"Leave it then," said Pierre. "I don't think it'll go any-where."

They decided to sleep. In case someone could see them from the entrance, they found spots deeper in the cave, cleared some rubble, and curled up.

The next morning they awoke to a roar of wings flap-ping. Looking up, Pierre saw hundreds of furry brown bats flying past them, entering the cave and flying beyond.

Andrew said, "Let's follow them."

"Don't you want to climb out and look around the out-side? How about that church?"

"We're down here now. And Pierre, people can live in caves. This is safe from Gulf hurricanes. We have to explore for the future."

"But, Andrew, is it safe from floods?"

Andrew didn't answer. It was as if the question had been a foolish one. But, Pierre thought, it wasn't foolish.

The glow of day brought only a little light to the cave, but that light was enough for the two to crouch, crawl, and squeeze until, half an hour later, they stood in a huge room.

There early morning light flowed through several holes in the round ceiling, which was covered with hanging bats.

All the little bat faces seemed to be angry. The animals protested the boys' visit with shrill chirping. Their teeth were bared like tiny bulldogs.

The cave continued, but the only way forward was along a high narrow ledge. A fall off the ledge could be fatal. They walked slowly, clinging to the wall. At some places the ledge was only inches wide. Pierre heard swift waters far below.

"A Mississippi River limestone cave," said Andrew. "I've heard about these." His whisper echoed. To Pierre an echo was like a cry that returned empty. It made him shiver.

After another half hour's walk, Pierre smelled a musty rotting odor. Stooping, the brothers stepped into a room stacked with white bones—not just a jumble of bones, but a pile of arm bones, a pile of leg bones, and blind-eyed skulls organized into a pyramid. Pierre whistled.

Andrew laughed. "I'm going back for our sack."

"You want a sack of bones?"

"For the pirates."

"Why? How will it help buy Isabel and Bella?" asked Pierre.

"We have to use everything we can find," said Andrew. "Those pirates are superstitious. Who knows how bones could help us?"

Andrew liked to scare people and play tricks on them. And sometimes those tricks made trouble. On the other hand, Pierre thought, his brother did seem to be thinking about their future.

As his brother crept back to climb out to the boat, Pierre studied the bones. All the skulls were large, with huge vacant eyespots. He hated their inviting stare.

"No," he whispered, holding his aching head, "I don't want to join you, but thanks just the same."

He glanced ahead. Light shone in from tree root holes all along the cave. The tunnel branched. One section dropped steeply, another went higher, and the middle tunnel went straight ahead.

I'll choose the one that goes up toward the surface, Pierre thought. Andrew can go wherever he wants.

After two hours, Andrew returned with both a sack and some Spanish moss. "To wrap the bones for silence," he explained. "I don't want them rattling."

"Make up a person, Gator Bait," said Pierre. "Two sets of arm bones, two sets of leg bones, hip bones, rib bones."

Together they assembled a tall body of bones, and then added some extra bones. "Which skull?" asked Andrew.

"The thickest and meanest looking," said Pierre.

Andrew hid the bag behind the pyramid of skulls, and to Pierre's surprise followed him along the rising tunnel. Through the damp limestone walls Pierre heard waters swishing. After a couple of miles more, the cave led to the surface. Andrew crawled out right away to explore under some live oaks heavy with Spanish moss.

Pierre lay in the cave exit thinking. The cave was about four miles long, he thought. The bones room had been about in the center. Walking and crawling, he was only about two hours from their pirogue.

His head throbbed, and he felt starved. Sitting up, he

placed a wad of damp moss on his forehead to soothe the headache. Just as he stood to follow his brother, he heard a whistle of danger.

He ducked back into the cave.

"Let go, let go of me!" Andrew yelled. His yell warned Pierre, who heard sounds of thumps and hard breathing.

"Who is it, Grandpapa?" asked a familiar voice.

"Methinks it's our chicken thief."

"He returned Picayune and his hens. Don't hurt the boy."

The man cackled in laughter. "The reward is mine!" he shouted. "Look at those eyes. Look at that dark skin. I have the Alexandre twins."

"Only one, Grandpapa."

"His brother is somewhere, Suzette. We'll smoke him out, and that reward is mine!"

chapter eleven

After he felt sure the Cajun grandpapa wasn't near the cave, Pierre crept up the tunnel to stare outside. Andrew sat bound in a chair in the middle of a sunny yard. Facing him, an old woman sat knitting on the porch of a shingle-roof wooden cabin.

The tiny house had a door in the front, and a window in front was shuttered. There was also a window near the roof and an outside ladder to the attic.

Did they expect him to run up to Andrew in the yard? Was this smoking the other twin out?

Apparently the family didn't know or didn't think about the cave. A singing Suzette pranced by hugging that black-and-white hen. Oh, for an egg to eat. Pierre felt dizzy and weak. His tongue felt swollen, his lips were cracked. He needed something to drink—water.

Take courage, he thought, and he crossed himself. After a while he saw the old woman bring a bowl to Andrew. While Suzette held a tin cup, the woman spooned red beans and rice into his mouth. From the cup Andrew drank deeply, and Pierre saw a creamy milk mustache on Andrew's brown face.

That could smoke him out! Those red beans and rice looked so good! Pierre wanted to run and beg for some.

I'll return to our boat and eat, he thought. Andrew was safe for now. The Cajun wouldn't take him anywhere without the second twin. Retracing his steps in the cave with bright daylight streaming through was easy, Pierre found. When he came to the narrow ledge, he tried to memorize the curves.

Rocks that had fallen on it were dangerous; he threw them into the water below. A clear ledge was safer, but he decided never to walk it in darkness. It just wasn't worth the risk.

Is that being a coward? he wondered. No, it was being wise, he decided. He hoped Andrew would be wise. Andrew worried him. He should have looked around before leaving the cave.

Walking back through the cave took a little less than two hours, faster than he had thought it would be. Once outside, Pierre climbed off the riverbank down to the pirogue, which hung like a hammock from tree roots.

The snails had all crawled out of the snail pail. Plucking them from the boat, he sucked and chewed, ate cattails, and drank deeply from river water. Yet even after he ate, his head ached from that fall. When he stared at his hands, he saw four hands instead of two. How could he rescue Andrew feeling as he did?

Where would they most likely keep Andrew? It was a small house, even for just three people. He bet Andrew would be kept in the attic.

Sitting in the pirogue, Pierre dipped Spanish moss in

the river, put it on his head, and leaned back to let it cool his aching forehead. He could remember a sinking feeling, then fuzzy darkness.

When he awoke, it was dark. He knew he hadn't fallen asleep; he had passed out. What should he do? Andrew needed help, and he, Pierre, needed time to recover.

He crept from the pirogue, checked the ropes still holding it securely, and walked on the riverbank. A cold breeze refreshed him at first, then he began shivering.

Footsteps. He ducked behind a live oak tree. The steps were coming toward him. He swung up into the tree and lay on a broad branch. His brown jacket and trousers were wonderful for hiding at night. If only he didn't pass out again and fall. He wrapped his legs around the tree limb.

The man was murmuring in Latin. How could he read in the dark? Breviary in hand, he was a priest reciting prayers. Pierre felt a jolt of joy. Here was help. Although priests preached obedience to masters, surely they were kindly men.

Reaching out to a branch, Pierre began to climb down. A second set of steps thudded on the ground. Pierre hung from the tree.

"*Père* Simone," said a voice that sounded excited, "Louis Bois has one twin of that marquis in New Orleans. He'll share the reward with the parish, *Père*, but we must all be on the lookout for the escaped slave's twin."

"*Merci, merci,* thank you," said the priest. "Tell Monsieur Bois I appreciate his thinking of the parish."

Swinging his leg back on the branch, Pierre rested his

throbbing head on the rough tree bark. It was clear! All by himself he would have to rescue his brother.

When the priest had strolled on, Pierre climbed down and walked back to the boat. He felt restless. Perhaps the bones would help in some way. Perhaps they would frighten the Cajuns? For now he would sleep.

The next morning he climbed the riverbank, slid down the rope, crawled and walked halfway through the cave until he reached the bag of bones. He added a couple of extra skulls to the bag and several long bones as well. Because caves sometimes held bones from a monastery, he looked around for crosses and candle wax. Why were these bones here?

In a corner he found his answer. A rotting pirate flag.

These were some pirate's store of bones. He shivered, and as he picked up the sack of bones, he wondered: If you "take courage," does that mean you choose it, and you're not afraid? Are only cowards afraid? Can people of courage be fearful?

Hand on the wall, he ran along that dangerous ledge in the cave. It was all familiar now. He tied the sack of bones on the end of the rope. After he climbed the rope, he hauled the bag like a bucket from a well. Dropping the rope back down into the cave, he stored the bones in the boat, then rested sitting by a tree for a while. The riverbank moved around and around. After a while the dizziness passed.

Sure now of what he must do, Pierre tied fresh grasses beside the pirogue and poled himself to harvest more snails.

He also reached and cut a new supply of cattail roots, then rapidly poled toward Hôtel de Jacques. Deep fog and mist would keep him hidden, he hoped.

After two hours he was off course. When he heard pirates singing in the mist, he recognized that he was going east. He swung to the west side of their island. Deep voices sang this song:

> "Sing of the salt of the seas,
> Brothers Bold,
> Gems and silks,
> Silvers and gold.
> Sing of the salt of the seas,
> Brothers Bold,
> It's treasure we seek,
> It's treasure we stole.
> Sing of the salt of the seas,
> Brothers Bold!"

The mist was thick enough in noonday's silvery light to hide him, but thin enough for him to follow the path he and Andrew had marked. Three hours later a flock of floating ducks parted to let him pass in the water. He smiled. They were his neighbors.

It was now the middle of the afternoon.

As soon as he reached Hôtel de Jacques, and had carried the bones and supplies inside, Pierre did something he had wanted to do for a long time. He let the big frogs drop into swamp waters and swim home. They must have families too, he thought. I want a big family. I want my brother, my mother, my little sister—all together. And more!

I will unite us, he thought. No, we will—Andrew and

I. Jacques freed us. Now it's up to us to free Isabel and Bella.

With a net he covered the creeping snails, and he dumped the cattails into their storage bucket. Next he cut rope long enough to reach up and into that attic, if need be. He stored it in the pirogue and added their old clothes from the marquis. Those clothes and shoes might help fool people.

When he stretched out on his bedroll, he felt lonely. What was Andrew thinking? How had he spent the night? What had he done all day?

That evening Pierre was truly bold. After a short rest, he poled his way toward the riverbank cave in the dark of the December evening three days after Christmas. He had to free Andrew. If it was about six o'clock when he left, he could be at the cave before midnight.

Take courage and hope in the Lord, he thought. Who had said that? Isabel! He remembered his mother whispering in his ear as she rocked him and Andrew once.

The night was more foggy than the day had been. Three hours later as Pierre passed the pirates, he heard them singing the "Dum dee dum" song, saw the light of their leaping yellow campfires, and sniffed smoky meat. The cheer of firelight made him feel more lonely.

Every so often he lay low and drifted, listening for other boats. Suddenly he heard water moving. A huge ship with a British flag sailed up beside him. He poled to hide under a bald cypress. The ship passed; he heard whispered orders.

The thin moon covered its face with a hood of clouds, and Pierre rapidly passed the ship in his pirogue and hurried toward the cave. It was not yet midnight. By the earth-works to the east he heard the Americans stirring. They must have been warned that the British were coming.

Two huge frigates flying American flags passed. Their sails used night breezes to glide in the fog. He poled more boldly. With a war going on, no one was looking for a boy in a pirogue. He ate some cattails. Chewing helped him breathe more slowly, kept his heart from jumping out of his throat.

Soon the ships began firing. The swamp reeled. Cannon fire flashed like horizontal lightning. The booming noise was worse than thunder. Ship masts cracked loudly, and ships' wood crunched. Pungent smoke made his eyes water.

People were gathered at the gray stone church to watch the battle. Pierre tied the pirogue in the security of the overhang and filled a bag with cattails to eat. He wound the rope on his shoulder.

Under cover of cannon and rifle fire, he scrambled up on the riverbank, then slid down the rope into the cave. Though he had vowed not to go through the cave in the dark, he moved ahead. He knew where he was going now, and he felt his way.

He crawled where the cave was low. When necessary to keep from hitting his head, he slid on his belly. As he came to the narrow ledge, he felt he was more sure now. Clearing the rocks had made it safer. He only hoped no other rocks had fallen to trip over. He actually ran in a crouch along the narrow ledge. In the bones room he paused to catch his breath. The path now led uphill to the surface. After two hours, he reached the other opening.

The ships were still at battle. At the cave opening he heard them loud again. In the dark he ran across the bog and leaned against the Cajun's home.

He whistled, and Andrew answered.

He followed his brother's whistle to the side of the cabin. Was this where Andrew was? Yes, another whistle came from the attic. Now, how could he get Andrew out?

chapter twelve

Was only Andrew up there? Was he tied to something? Picking up a pebble, Pierre threw it in the yard. No one responded. He threw a handful. They rattled against a tin washbasin. Surely that would raise someone? He hoped everyone but Andrew was somewhere watching the battle.

Pierre waited patiently. Rifles and muskets exchanged fire with cannons. Then the booming cannons were silent, but the swamp was aglow. He felt something by his leg. It was the hen. He picked it up, stuck his nose in its warm, sweet-smelling feathers, and put it down. Enough time had passed.

He picked up a good-sized stone, tied it onto his rope, and tossed it through the window into the attic. He enjoyed a moment of pride as stone and rope flew up and dropped inside. He had done it in one silent toss.

Was his brother free to escape? He felt a jerk on the line, and soon Andrew climbed over the windowsill and dropped by Pierre's side.

As he dropped, two men with lanterns ran from around the sides of the house. "*Voilà*," shouted the Cajun grandpapa.

"*Voilà*," shouted the other man. Together they ran at the boys. Pierre and Andrew crouched and waited. Each knew what the other would do. All their lives had prepared them for this moment. From childhood, they had always escaped this way.

Pierre glanced around. Anyone else? Only two old men? Picking up the speckled hen, he stroked the feathers and whispered, "Sorry." When the men ran up and reached out for them, Pierre saw Andrew bend down and run off at knee level toward one man.

Pierre then threw his hen in the men's faces, bent and ran in the opposite direction. This was their childhood strategy. They always ran in opposite directions. With one person chasing, only one twin could be caught at a time. By the time the chaser turned for the second twin, the first had struggled free.

Behind him Pierre heard the Cajun and his friend bump into the wall. They seemed blinded by chicken claws and feathers. He hoped Suzette's hen wasn't injured.

Tonight the chase was more serious. This time they weren't little boys running because the marquis had called for them. They were running for freedom, and there were two men chasing, not one.

Pierre wasted no time circling to the cave and crawling in the entrance. His brother was there seconds later. As they scrambled deeper and deeper into the safety of the cave, he heard the men's angry shouts.

Deep in the jet blackness of the cave Andrew began to hesitate, but Pierre took his hand and guided him. By now Pierre felt he knew every turn. Pressing Andrew against the wall, he led him along the ledge. His brother trembled, but Pierre felt surefooted.

At the cave opening near their pirogue, a glow of light shone down. Andrew climbed the rope to get out and slid back down. "There are fire and people on the riverbank," he said. "We better hide here."

Glancing up at the glow, Pierre frowned. Should they wait? It was probably near six in the morning now. The battle had ended, but people on the riverbank were still watching a fire.

"No," he said, "we go now while it's still dark. Everyone is busy watching. They don't know you escaped yet."

They climbed out and freed the pirogue.

"*Père,*" someone called from the crowd. "Two hooded boys. Do you think?" Pierre glanced toward them.

"No," said the priest, "those are boys I know. Monsieur Bois has the twins of the marquis."

Pierre grinned. The priest had helped them after all! Would he have helped before? Maybe, but slavery was legal. The law said runaway slave property had to be returned.

Besides, Pierre thought, he hadn't needed help. He had saved Andrew by himself. He grinned in silent triumph. They poled away with no one else challenging them. In fact someone in a boat called "Ahoy," and Pierre waved.

With both of them pushing poles, they slid rapidly toward the glow. It would be in their path. "A ship is on fire," said Andrew. He faced the fire; Pierre poled from the back of the boat.

"American or British?"

"American. I read *Carolina*," Andrew said. "We have to go around it." Andrew shifted direction.

"No," Pierre said, digging his pole into the bottom. "That's the long way. We'll use the fire for light. I don't think anyone's interested in a couple of hooded boys in a boat."

Andrew turned to look at Pierre. "You must have been so afraid," he said. "I know you must have cried."

Pierre opened his mouth and stared at his brother, then closed his mouth. Who was his brother talking about? Plans for Andrew's escape and his aching head had been his concerns.

Andrew caught his shoulder and held Pierre to the light. "Your face is dark with bruises. You have a lump on your forehead."

Pierre shrugged and said, "From the fall. And you're right, I missed you." Andrew hadn't even said thanks for the rescue, but Pierre didn't need thanks. He felt wonderful.

As they poled nearer the blazing ship, Pierre heard splashing and screams. He poled toward one man, but the thrashing soldier was pulled under by an alligator.

"These American soldiers are being eaten alive," he called. "We have to help them."

"There's another soldier fighting an alligator," Andrew whispered. "We should pass and get to safety. Quick, pole this way."

"We can't leave people to die!" Pierre stared at his brother. What a time for Andrew to think about safety! "You saw that man and the alligator? We have to help. With our pirogue, we're the only ones here who can save them!"

"We have to think about ourselves," Andrew said. "Someone could capture us. We better pole away." He dug in his pole.

"We can't leave people to die," shouted Pierre. "Even if we're caught," he added in a low voice.

Andrew sighed. "We could be sorry."

They poled over, grabbed a young man's arm, and pulled him out of the water. "Climb in," said Pierre.

"Thank you mighty much, Son."

They let him off on a narrow strip of land and returned for another soldier. "Thank you, lads, I can't swim a lick," shouted the man.

They alternated poling and pulling into the pirogue sailors and soldiers who were jumping from the burning ship *Carolina*. Some could swim to shore, others couldn't. Since the pirogue was small, they ferried them to land one or two at a time. It was frantic work. One soldier's hand was torn and bleeding. Another had been burned in the fire. All the time the twins tried to keep their hoods pulled forward.

When they had helped the last soldier they could find climb onshore, Pierre tossed their old dancing clothes onto a cypress shrub. At last he was free of old shoes and clothes. He hoped the clothes would free them too.

A man in uniform and long dark cloak strode to the edge of the land to stare at them. Pierre had seen him in the distance watching them haul people from the swamp. His face was thin and seemed cast in harsh stone.

"It's General Andrew Jackson," whispered Andrew, his voice cracking in excitement. "I saw him once in New Orleans."

Resting on his pole, Pierre stared at the tall, thin man. This general had been training freed colored men to fight. There were whole areas of New Orleans where freed people of African ancestry worked at trades. Other leaders of the army and navy wouldn't accept them, but General Jackson treated them fairly. He told them they could help defend their city of New Orleans.

The marquis had gone to the general with Governor Claiborne to protest colored troops, but General Jackson hadn't changed his mind. Pierre liked him for that.

When Andrew threw back his hood and stood to salute, Pierre stood beside him. He used the pole to keep from toppling.

General Andrew Jackson returned their salute. "Thank you," he said. Pierre watched the general stroll over, pick their old clothes off the shrub, and walk away.

"What were those?" asked Andrew.

"Our old clothes."

"Now he knows who we are," Andrew said. "When he returns to New Orleans, he'll tell the marquis that we're here. They'll come after us. See what you did?" He hit Pierre.

"I hadn't planned on that," Pierre said. He had wanted to make people believe they had drowned, and now that wouldn't work. What a mistake! The clothes would prove that they were very much alive!

And in nine or ten days someone would have to begin the journey through the swamp, up the Mississippi River, and through the city of New Orleans to buy Isabel and Bella. It all seemed so impossible.

chapter thirteen

When they arrived that night at Hôtel de Jacques, before Andrew was finished tying up the pirogue, Pierre was asleep on his bedroll.

The next morning his brother had to shake him awake. "Pierre," he whispered, "how did our skeleton bones get here?"

Pierre asked, "How do you think?" He turned over.

"But they were here before we arrived last night."

Now Pierre rubbed his eyes and sat up. He looked at his brother. "So?"

Andrew's mouth hung open. "Hen Heart, you mean to say you came back to Hôtel de Jacques all by yourself? You brought these bones here? You harvested these snails? You cut lengths of rope?" He shook his head in disbelief.

Hungry at the mention of snails, Pierre pulled the pail over. Uncovering them, he chose a fat, juicy one.

Andrew stared through the branches toward the velvety green leaves of Lettuce Lake. "The marquis used to tell me mean things about you," he said. "That you were a lazy liar. He told me that you made fun of me and hated me." He shook his head. "Before life here, I felt I never knew you even though we were twins."

"I think he tried to make us enemies of each other," said Pierre. "He didn't want slave brothers to care for each other."

"Remember," Andrew said, "sometimes he would keep us apart for days. And we would find a way to steal time together at night."

"He made our dance master teach us separately. And I can never forget the day he sold Isabel away from us."

"He told me she was just loaned out to work," Andrew said. "He promised me she would be back. Then months later when she didn't return, he told me Isabel didn't want to come back. That she didn't love us anymore." He leaned against the wall. "I felt awful. Abandoned by my own mother!"

"He told you that?" Pierre struck the floor with a fist. "From the first day, he told me Isabel was sold and that I'd never see her again." He dropped his blanket from his shoulders. "I was so angry because you wouldn't believe that she was sold."

"And I was so angry with you for not believing that she *would* return," Andrew said. "No wonder we couldn't agree on anything. The marquis set us against each other. He said you were weak and dumb, but you aren't."

"I was furious because you were so bullheaded and stubborn. I didn't know what the marquis had told you." Pierre took deep breaths. "Andrew," he said, "the marquis tried to make us hate each other. Well, he won't succeed." Andrew didn't answer.

Frowning, Pierre stared out the walls. A soft morning breeze blew the Spanish moss to sway like curtains at a window. An egret with broad white wings glided past. Frog pip-ings grew shrill with sunrise; and as the brothers talked, the sun began to burn off the fog. Two green lizards ran over Pierre's blanket. He shivered.

Was their fire still alive? He stumbled to his feet. Yes. Adding dry straw a blade at a time, Pierre blew the embers.

"We are brothers, and even closer—we're twins," he told Andrew. "Now we work together." He put water on to boil.

"Yes," said Andrew, "and we have friends."

"What friends?"

"Remember Suzette? The little girl who loves chickens even more than you do?"

"How could I forget?"

"She was guarding me when you came. When she heard me answer you with a whistle, she pulled a fish knife from a basket." Andrew smiled. "At first I was afraid, but she used the knife to cut the ropes holding me. She helped me tie the rope you threw up there so I could slide down it."

"She helped you? How were you tied?"

"Hands and feet to a chair," said Andrew. He raised his eyebrows. "Maybe she could help us buy Isabel?"

Pierre shook his head. "How could a child younger than we are buy slaves at an auction?"

Frowning, Andrew peered in the frog bucket. "What happened? Did we eat the last frog?"

"Let's eat snails," Pierre said with a sigh. "They don't have sad eyes like a frog."

"That's good," said Andrew. "I never liked killing those frogs. Cleaning fish is different. What else do we do today?"

Pierre smiled in relief. Andrew wasn't so different after all. What else did they need to do? "Our clothes are dirty from bat droppings and crawling in the dirt." Pierre lifted his jacket and looked at the sharp-smelling white smudges.

"I think we need more than one set of clothes," said Andrew with a yawn. "Then I won't have to wait for my clothes to dry."

A couple of days later the twins' new outfits were almost done. They were cut from a dark green bolt of cloth Jacques had left them. This time Pierre cut patch pockets for both trousers and jackets. Their hoods were deep again.

That morning Andrew climbed down from the third floor. "We need to harvest extra supplies." He had been hemming pants.

"Why?" asked Pierre. He sat cross-legged finishing a pocket.

"The British are bringing up big guns from the Gulf. They're hidden behind casks on their ships, but from above I can see the guns."

"What does that mean for us?"

"A big battle is ahead. The earthworks must be over a mile long now. They'll be fighting again soon."

Pierre moaned. "I hate all that noise."

"The sound of battle is rally rousing," said Andrew. He rubbed his hands together.

"Not for the people who're injured or killed," Pierre muttered. Andrew and he would always be different in some ways, he supposed.

"Hurry and finish. The pirates are probably gone," Andrew said. "After we store supplies, we can visit there. We'll leave them some footsteps of fox fire and bones to make a skeleton. Maybe we can scare them away and live on that island."

Pierre shivered. Should they go again? he wondered. Had their father sailed and laughed with those very same men? And was their father really dead?

He had barely known Jacques, Pierre thought. He felt he should grieve, but how could he grieve for someone he hardly knew? Glancing around at Hôtel de Jacques, suddenly he did feel sorrow. This was his father's gift. Their father had built a hiding place to ensure their freedom. Pierre felt tears in his eyes.

With sorrow came anger. How dare those pirates kill his father! This time he wouldn't mind helping Andrew fool them. Maybe the skeleton would haunt their sleep.

"Do you think they killed Jacques?" Pierre asked.

"Could be," said his brother. "Where's that moldy bread flour he left us?"

"Would I love a crust of bread," said Pierre, handing him the sack of pink and green flour.

Andrew cleared his throat. "At that Cajun's cabin I had bacon, ham, egg omelette, bread, red beans, rice." He sighed. "I'm sorry you didn't get any."

"You bet I'm sorry too!"

They laughed. Andrew divided the flour and gave Pierre half in a bag. "This may help save us sometime," he said. "Pirates may be afraid of powders. Other superstitious people are."

"Wait, what day is this?" asked Pierre. He counted notches from their calendar. "Tomorrow is New Year's Day."

His brother frowned. "Time is so different in the swamp. Is today New Year's Eve? I suppose the new year will be 1815. Aunt Berniece will be making New Year's resolutions."

"Me too. I resolve to have a family this year."

"You mean, you want to free Isabel and Bella for family?"

"I've been thinking," Pierre said. He stopped sewing and stared out the woven wall. "You know, we have lots of Jacques's diamonds and rubies, probably his share from many pirate trips. They aren't any use to us. Why don't we buy everyone's freedom at that slave auction?"

"How do you know they'll accept jewels? Who'll go to buy them?"

"People buy their loved ones free all the time. Maybe we could even live in New Orleans with our family," said Pierre, but he knew it was a daydream. He jabbed the cloth with his needle and thread.

"Trouble is, we can't buy ourselves free," Andrew said. "The marquis will never let us go. He loved our dance. Face it, we're escaped slaves with a price on our heads!"

Pierre shook his head and shrugged. "It was just an idea."

Poling their boat through the swamp, they harvested food all morning. When they pulled into rushes by the pirates' island, it was late afternoon. Pierre jerked old grasses loose. "Gator Bait," he said, "we need to look like these darker rushes."

From the sea of grass they pulled out sections to draw

through the rope around the boat, making a sort of grass skirt.

"Our pirogue looks like an island of grass. Why don't we leave it here and splash over?" asked Andrew.

Pierre stared into the still water. "Alligators swim really fast," he said. "And it may be deeper than you think."

"We swim well."

"No splashing. We can't make any noise."

"But the pirates are all gone," said Andrew. "You can see that. We don't need to stay quiet."

"Maybe," said Pierre, "but the bones. We can't swim fast carrying bones." He was relieved to have an excuse. It was hard to keep Andrew from doing something foolish.

"We could tie the pirogue to that tree and take a chance," Andrew said.

Nodding, Pierre poled toward the island. They attached the back of the boat to a cypress knee, and Pierre tossed Spanish moss inside the boat just in case someone looked down. Even so, he felt uneasy.

Bones over his shoulder, Andrew ran for the place where the treasure trunk had been. If that was what he was after, Pierre thought, they still had no right to that gold. He hung back and listened. A sound bothered him, a sound made by neither bird nor insect nor any other animal. Worried, he shimmied up the tree trunk and stood on a branch to look over the island.

A snoring pirate! He whistled danger.

Andrew stood still, then looked all about until he spied the sleeping man too. Pierre watched him begin to tiptoe forward. But he should have run back! Didn't he know how dangerous it was?

Yet as he watched, Pierre saw Andrew assemble a person from the bones, then make fox fire steps. Fortunately the pirate snored on. Andrew continued his work until he stopped and stared in another direction, then whistled to Pierre. Another sleeping pirate! Yet even then Andrew didn't stop.

Pierre began to wonder if he was a coward after all. He couldn't make himself move out of the tree. He had wanted to revenge Jacques's death by haunting the pirates with fox fire and the skeleton, but now he only wanted to escape.

He watched Andrew haul the bag of extra bones up a tree and leave it hanging over the place where the pirates ate. The rope was tied so the sack was hidden in moss and leaves.

Just as his brother began to run back, the pirate near Pierre raised his head. Just what he had been afraid would happen!

Pierre whistled to warn Andrew.

Across the island Andrew sank down among leafy brush. The pirate rose, relieved himself at the tree where Pierre was hidden, and walked to stir the campfires. He hummed, then began singing:

> "Oh, it's of the pirate life I sing,
> And pirate treasure home I bring.
> Wild and free, before the breeze,
> A life of song, adventure, ease.
> Them that fight us, drown in chains,

Spill blood and guts, for their pains,
Let this be warning, to take care,
For pirates promise none to spare."

And then Pierre heard the rowing of a longboat. The pirates were back! He and Andrew were trapped. Pierre felt weak and trembly. Andrew's mischief had gotten them into trouble. Deadly trouble!

chapter fourteen

The pirates jumped out of their longboat and sloshed to shore. They would be marching near the bushes where Andrew hid.

For a moment Pierre closed his eyes. No, he thought, Andrew needs me to be alert. His hands patted his flour bag.

Andrew had been right. They might need to use the flour to get away from the pirates. But why had they come in the first place? It was foolish, and he was supposed to be the wise twin! From now on he had to make better decisions.

The sun's low rays gilded the swamp waters. A flock of egrets flapped past, screeching. They were followed by honking gray geese stretching wide wings toward the clouds.

"Lafitte got us all pardoned," called one pirate to the two who had remained behind. Three other longboats landed men, until there were about thirty in all. Swords and pistols at their sides, they tramped onto shore talking and laughing.

"Break out the rum," the red-haired pirate called.

Pierre raised his eyebrows; there was hope after all. If the pirates got drunk, he and Andrew could escape. Darkness would be their cover.

"No rum," shouted Evil Eye Alex. "There's a battle tonight, or tomorrow for sure. None of you rascals can be drunk. General Jackson needs our ammunition and our numbers."

The pirates shouted in reply:

"Why are we fighting their chuckle-headed battle?"

"I don't need no pardon. Nobody caught me yet."

"It's our ammunition, we stole it. Are those hen-hearted numskulls paying us?"

"Let them sniveling puppies fight their own war!"

Evil Eye laughed and pulled a loaf of bread from a sack. Pierre licked his lips and took a deep breath. The sack was full of long brown loaves. He had just sniffed the warm yeast smell when he heard a scream.

"Black Jack returned!" The words were muffled with horror. Pirates snatched pistols, or drew swords, and ran toward the scream.

So they did kill him, thought Pierre. Tears filled his eyes. They killed our father, and now they feel guilty.

"It's only a skeleton," called Evil Eye. "Skeletons don't have names."

"This skeleton has a name," called a bearded black pirate. "There's his signature as good as you could find on parchment."

What was it? Pierre leaned forward, reached to grab a tree limb, and missed. He snapped back, but Spanish moss fell. He glanced around. None of the pirates seemed to have noticed. Slowly, silently, Pierre climbed higher in the tree.

Glancing across, he saw Andrew take advantage of the distraction of the skeleton to climb into a tree on his side of the island. Good for him.

Pierre had never felt so helpless. They were trapped, but they hadn't been seen yet. If only they could hide until the pirates went to sleep. If only they could escape to their pirogue safely.

"Our Jolly Roger!" a pirate yelled. He waved flags, the ones from Jacques's trunk. "Black Jack had the new flags."

Had Andrew hung the flags over the skeleton? Pierre was glad the pirates were frightened. Pressing his back against the tree trunk, he breathed out slowly.

"Footsteps of fire!" yelled another pirate pointing to earth. The sun had gone down, and with the descent of darkness, the fox fire could be seen.

As the pirates began arguing about footsteps and flags, a pirate ran over to Pierre's tree. The one-eared man unbuttoned his trousers. This must be where they relieve themselves, Pierre thought. A split-tail swallow flew past, saw Pierre, and flew into the dusk with a chirp of friendly surprise. The pirate glanced up, pointed, and screamed:

"There's the sniveling puppy!"

The pirate's call wasn't noticed at first, but the one-eared man kept pointing to Pierre. I wish I could disappear, thought Pierre. The man kept shouting. Two pirates ran toward One Ear, and the others were looking his way. Time to do something and quick, thought Pierre.

Remembering what his brother had said about superstitious people and powders, he pulled out the bag of moldy flour and sprinkled flour on old One Ear.

Beating his clothes, the pirate screamed, "Poison powder!"

Pierre lifted the bag high and covered himself with white powdery flour. He rubbed clumps of pink and green along his hands, then tucked the bag of flour in his pocket.

The gang of pirates ran near. He waited until they were under the tree, jabbering and pointing at him. Behind them there was a clear space. He somersaulted over their heads into the clearing.

Then Pierre danced as he had never danced before. The marquis and company would have been hypnotized. His powdered hood was forward, his floured hands moved from his sides to the front and back again. Feet raised then lowered, he danced slowly as if he were a cloud drifting. The pirates drew back from him. They were so silent, he could hear them breathing.

All the time he sprinkled flour in his path. He had circled the camp and begun another trip when Andrew reached out to pull on his jacket. Pierre stopped with one foot raised. From the corner of his eye he saw Andrew, also covered with flour, in step behind him. He heard Andrew's feet thump on the ground, heard his hard breathing. Pierre danced forward. They were dancing in perfect rhythm.

His brother's dance was to the same beat, but from the corner of his eye Pierre saw Andrew sprinkle his hood with flour from time to time. Pierre did the same, but slowly. The pirates were all silent and staring. Not one of them moved, except to draw back when Andrew danced too near.

The mother dog sat wagging its tail. The puppies pranced playfully, but didn't come near them. Soon Andrew whistled a signal to change the dance, and Pierre followed him.

I remember this dance, Pierre thought. After round-offs, and skip steps, he's coming to the point where I dance across from him, and we leave together from the marquis's drawing room door. That might work, it just might work.

Pierre danced in, danced across Andrew and out. Should they leave together as the dance called for, or separate to escape? He couldn't see Andrew's face, but his brother was swinging the dance around so they would exit where the boat lay. Should they give away where the pirogue was? Should he let Andrew lead him?

They reached the point where he danced away from Andrew. His heart beat faster. Why was Andrew still going in the opposite direction? The rope, the rope! Andrew was going to pull the rope. Pierre danced in little circles opposite his brother's circles. Had Andrew done it?

They danced closer, somersaulted twice. Andrew tossed his sack of flour; seconds later Pierre tossed his in the same way. They dance-stepped through brush and around trees. Skipped on cypress knees and jumped into the pirogue. No sound behind them. The pirates weren't following.

When he thought of those cocked pistols and sharp swords, Pierre began to tremble. He dipped his pole and pushed. The brothers sat on the pirogue floor and ever so slowly pushed their boat to drift away. Pierre hoped they looked like a clump of floating rushes. Were the pirates watching? Would they follow?

If they wished, the pirates could overtake them any second. Several men rowing a longboat sometimes moved faster than a ship under sail. Pierre dared not speak. Were they going to pull it off?

Suddenly he heard a shout from the pirates' island. Pierre heard the pirates yelling and racing around. Evil Eye was calling them, shouting orders, but he was drowned by the screams.

What had happened?

Andrew laughed. "I thought that sack of extra bones would never fall!"

It seemed like hours since Andrew had danced over to that rope. But now the distraction of the bones, so long delayed, might help them still.

Maybe and maybe not! Pierre glanced over his shoulder. Someone was rowing rapidly toward them. "A boat," he whispered. They weren't free yet.

chapter fifteen

The men rowing rapidly toward them were not pirates. Pierre could hear but not see. Who were they?

"Ahoy," said a voice in British accent. "Who goes?" All the men seemed dressed alike and, although he couldn't see in the dark, Pierre suspected that the uniforms had red jackets. He heard a musket click.

"Ahoy," he said. He and Andrew were poling the boat mightily, but the bottom of the swamp sank. Now they had to extend their poles for roots or grass to push against. The pirogue slowed down. They were trapped.

"Who goes?" The longboat rowed directly across them.

Pierre's scalp tingled, and he felt a crawling sensation at the back of his neck. After escaping the pirates, they couldn't be captured by the British. He had to think of something. Yes! He knew what to say. His heart was pounding.

"Beauty and booty," he said in as low a voice as he could manage.

Immediately the longboat turned and rowed away. Andrew patted Pierre's shoulder, and Pierre made a fist in triumph. They were free. In silence they headed for Hôtel de Jacques.

On New Year's Day Pierre slept until noon. Several times he heard Andrew muttering from the third-story lookout, but he refused to wake up. When a sunbeam tickled his eyelid, he rolled over and yawned.

Andrew whistled.

Pierre sat up. After stepping into his trousers, and pulling on his green jacket, he climbed up to sit beside his brother. In the strong sunlight, he could see for miles and miles.

The swamp had traffic like downtown Canal Street in New Orleans. He saw sailing ships and longboats with redcoats. He saw colorful pirates, plain-coated Americans, and Cajun fishermen. Men and boys swarmed over the earthworks.

"The British ships are lining up by the earthworks," Andrew said. He handed Pierre the telescope.

Pierre frowned. Andrew seemed to enjoy this preparation for battle; Pierre couldn't stomach it. When he looked through the telescope, he saw that the British ships had pulled up sideways to the earthworks. Their cannons shot broadside, but American cannons could put holes broadside in the ships too.

Boom. The first British cannon began the battle. Soon cannon booms, musket fire, and rifle *tat, tat, tats* tore away their green kingdom's peace. Pierre climbed down the ladder.

Sitting on his bedroll, he closed his eyes and hugged

his knees. Andrew had been smart to store provisions before this battle. Nervous songbirds hid in their cypress tree under hanging moss; ducks took refuge in Lettuce Lake. Dagger-tooth dragged a duck underwater for lunch, and Pierre shivered.

After a couple of hours, Andrew dropped down. His pale gray eyes were big. "Those casks in front of the big guns all split, and the gunners were hit. British ships are sailing away, and the Americans are dancing on top of the earthworks." Andrew reached for a snail.

Turning away, Pierre felt sick.

Suddenly he saw a hand on their floor. He whistled, but it came out like a lisp. He couldn't believe his eyes. How could they not have heard or seen someone below? In the excitement of battle they hadn't been watching.

As he stared, the man's hand reached up from the first story room below. Slowly the man hoisted himself through the trapdoor without using the ladder. Black hair, broad shoulders. With a graceful jump, Evil Eye stood in their home. He pulled a bag through the floor opening.

"Ahoy, boys."

Pierre was more shocked than afraid.

Raising his hand, Andrew said, "Ahoy."

Evil Eye pushed his eye patch up. Two pale blue eyes smiled at them. His wavy black hair hung over his shoulders like a horse's tail. He was sleek and muscular and, for a pirate, he was outstanding in that his ears, nose, fingers, and feet were all intact.

From head to toe he was dressed in purple: a full-sleeved blousy purple shirt, purple vest, coarsely woven purple trousers, and soft-kid knee-boots dyed purple. His broad sash, knotted on the side, was purple. To Pierre he looked like a man who had been held by the ears and dipped to his chin in a purple grape-juice vat.

The pirate rubbed his hands and glanced around as if seeking somewhere to sit. He paced the room, stared out the basketlike walls. Pierre was frozen in fascination.

"Black Jack built a fine hideaway," Evil Eye said. "Took me ages to find it. If that ship's line hadn't been down. . . ."

In a blink, Pierre jumped down the ladder to pull up the first floor rope. He was usually so careful. What had he been thinking? He glanced out the trapdoor and saw a longboat. Everything else looked all right, nothing taken, no other pirates near. Climbing slowly, he returned to Andrew and Evil Eye. As he passed the pirate's bag by the trapdoor, he couldn't help sniffing.

"Yes," said Evil Eye, "here's bread." From his bag he pulled some loaves like those they had seen the day before. He broke one and handed half to each of them.

"Thank you, sir." Pierre remembered his manners and waved to his bed. "Won't you have a seat, sir?"

The pirate sat on the bedroll, back against the wall, long legs stretched out before him. Pierre and Andrew sat cross-legged on the floor. Pierre was so hungry for bread that he chewed and chewed. The outside was hard with a shiny tan crust; the inside was soft and wheaty.

"Fine trickery you sneaking puppy rascals played on us."

Pierre winced.

Evil Eye wiped his lips. "You boys," he said slowly, as if

apologizing for his crude words, "you boys danced like . . . fine young men."

"Thank you," Andrew said.

Pierre bit off more bread. The golden crust was crunchy and sweet.

"You are surviving well," said Evil Eye, glancing around. "From sons of Black Jack, I would expect no less." He grinned. "And I," with a flourish he placed an arm across his chest and bowed, "I am your uncle. Jacques and I were half brothers. He was born to a slave woman, I was born to our father's wife, and only two days apart."

Of course! From the moment he saw him, Pierre had felt this man looked familiar. He looked like Jacques. Here was someone they could ask about Jacques. And maybe this uncle would help them free Isabel and Bella. He grew excited.

"Do you know what happened to Jacques?" Pierre asked. "He was supposed to return weeks ago."

Evil Eye shook his head. "Methinks he's in a watery grave, boys. Them around me seemed mighty fearful of his ghost." He sighed.

"He was going to buy Isabel and our little sister," said Pierre. "They're to be sold in a January ninth slave auction." Pierre's voice cracked. "We need our mother now more than ever."

Evil Eye nodded. "Many a night Black Jack sang her praises. He planned all this," the pirate waved at the hideaway, "to fool the marquis. He hated that man."

The pirate sighed. "Three years ago when the Marquis De Ville sold Isabel, Jacques almost went insane. He howled, tore his hair, wept for days on end. Three years he took to build this tree house. His share of the loot was to buy her free."

Evil Eye went on: "He managed to free the two of you. Yes, and he probably returned for Isabel, the hen-hearted numskull." Evil Eye wiped his lips again and sat staring out the walls. Pierre could swear there were tears in his pale blue eyes.

Andrew added straw to their fire. Pierre climbed down for the tea tin and fresh water. Soon the water bubbled merrily. They put tea leaves in a cup for Evil Eye. Pierre offered him snails, cattails, and a cup of tea.

"Good pleasure, boys," said Evil Eye. He sipped tea like a gentleman.

Thoughts danced in Pierre's head. Should he ask Evil Eye to help them? After all, the pirate was his uncle.

Could he trust a pirate? Best to test him.

"Did you play with Jacques when you were boys?" he asked.

chapter sixteen

Evil Eye chuckled and ate a snail. The sun blinked once on the watery horizon, and it was dark. By the flicker of fire, Pierre stared at Evil Eye.

"As I said," the pirate told them, "we were born two days apart. Jacques was born first, and Jacques's mother nursed him at one breast and me at the other. We grew up and were tutored together." He snorted and shook his head.

"Poor Jacques. My father treats his slaves like regular servants. Jacques only realized he was a slave—our father's property—when he fell in love with Isabel. After they were married, the Marquis De Ville refused to sell, free, or release her. Only then did Jacques realize that he had no rights."

Pierre noticed that his grandfather was still alive. There was family; they had a grandfather! Maybe he could help? But what kind of man would keep his son a slave?

"The ghost eyes go on." Evil Eye chuckled. "Our father has those pale gray eyes. Jacques had gray eyes, and Isabel's are light brown, I hear. You boys got a double dose of light eyes."

Andrew asked, "Why do you cover your eye if it's not blind?" The pirate's eye patch clung to the side of his forehead like a four-legged spider.

"To strike terror! Pirates rule by fear. Pale blue eyes make a man look weak. Use a patch and take the name of Evil Eye, and a man gets feared." He laughed loudly, coarsely.

Pierre put a finger to his lips. The pirate was talking louder than they ever did. Evil Eye lowered his voice and glanced around.

"Yes," said the pirate in a softer voice. "We played together, Jacques and I. But after he married, Jacques grew bitter. The marquis only allowed occasional visits with Isabel. Even when our father freed Jacques, Jacques was not happy."

How could a man have kept his son a slave at all? Pierre wondered again.

There were many things Pierre wanted to know. About his grandfather. About a slave grandmother. He opened his mouth to speak, but Andrew asked:

"Who became a pirate first?"

That was not what Pierre would have asked. He tore off another chunk of bread.

Head tossed back, Evil Eye laughed softly, but crudely. Was coarse crude laughter another way of striking terror?

"One day," the pirate said, waving an arm, "Jean Lafitte was challenged to a pistol duel at dawn by Lake Pontchartrain. I was his second, but he tricked the man, a count. He had Jacques jam the count's pistol." Evil Eye laughed as if it were a great joke.

"Our father heard about it and disowned us, both of us. We lost our inheritance." He frowned, then shrugged.

"We celebrated that night at the Inn of Twelve Sisters.

Because we knew the truth about the count's death, the two of us were a threat to Lafitte. It was join him or die. Without much trouble Jean Lafitte talked us into joining him on the account."

Pierre wondered what "on the account" meant.

Evil Eye answered his raised eyebrows. "Every pirate goes 'on the account.' You see, there's no pay until we rob a ship. Then every man gets a shift of clothes and a share of the booty. Of course, the captain and quartermaster get two shares each. Boatswain and gunner one and a half. All the crew get one share."

"That's fair," said Andrew, nodding. "What keeps pirates from stealing from each other?"

Pierre glanced toward Jacques's trunk. Had he stolen?

"If a pirate robs another pirate, he loses an ear, a finger or hand, a foot or nose, sometimes his life."

Pierre watched his brother sit straighter. Andrew wasn't smiling anymore.

"Thing is," Evil Eye said with a sigh, "there's punishment for robbing, but none for murder." He took a sip of tea. "Fewer crew, bigger share. They kill among the Brotherhood all the time. With Black Jack dead, every man will get more loot from that last ship we sank."

Pierre glanced at Andrew. His brother looked a little green. He climbed down the ladder to use the toilet.

When he returned, Pierre asked, "Who is our grandfather?"

Evil Eye looked at him.

"Your father, our grandfather," said Pierre, leaning forward.

"You don't know?"

Would he ask if he did? "No, sir."

"He's Prince Andrew Pierre Alexandre. I haven't seen him in years. I'm not welcome at home since he cut me from his will."

"He never came to the marquis's drawing room," said Pierre, "but I had heard of Prince Alexandre of Burgundy."

"Of course. He wouldn't have been invited," said the pirate. "The prince and the marquis are enemies. The marquis hates our father, and our father returns the favor."

"We were named after the prince," said Andrew.

Pierre realized he had almost forgotten their purpose. And Evil Eye did seem loyal to Jacques. "Can you help us buy Isabel? We have diamonds and rubies here." He pointed to Jacques's trunk.

With a strange look in his eyes, Evil Eye stood, then knelt by the trunk. "It's safe," said Pierre. "We opened it and took out all the daggers and swords."

In spite of Pierre's assurance, the pirate leaned back as he gingerly lifted the lid to the trunk. With trembling hands he ran fingers through the gems. His lips were parted and he was staring.

Pierre said, "We have nice clothes for a merchant gentleman that would fit you. There they are." He lifted a black velvet cloak and white silk shirt from the pile behind the trunk. He was thinking that in merchant clothes and without an eye patch, Evil Eye Alex could look decent enough to go and buy Isabel and Bella.

"Black Jack stole from Jean Lafitte," said the pirate in

a whisper. "These gem settings are diamonds in *fleur-de-lis*, and rubies in crowns. These were hidden in a house somewhere, I think, and no one was supposed to know where they were. When Lafitte finds these missing, it's every man on guard for his life!"

The pirate was trembling all over now. He closed the trunk lid with shaky hands. Pierre couldn't believe that this ferocious uncle would tremble with fear. Pirates were supposed to be brave. Evil Eye peered around. He pulled his eye patch to cover an eye, a different eye this time, and backed over to the floor opening.

"Don't, don't," he stuttered, pointing to the jewels.

"Don't use them?" Pierre asked. "Who will know in the city? Couldn't we send them with a buyer?"

"No. No. No! Those are gems from Napoleon's treasury. Jewel merchants would know them anywhere."

"How can you help us then, Uncle?" asked Pierre.

With clumsy feet, Evil Eye was backing down the ladder. "If I were you boys, I'd dump that trunk in the swamp. Don't be caught with Lafitte's. . . ."

Pierre followed him down the ladder. Opening the trapdoor, Evil Eye slid down the rope and splashed before climbing into the longboat. Pierre saw Dagger-tooth hopefully lift its nose from Lettuce Lake.

Help had seemed so near, Pierre thought, and now this uncle was abandoning them. "Help us for Jacques's sake," he called. "We need you, Uncle."

The oars dipped and swished unsteadily. The pirate couldn't seem to reach a smooth rowing rhythm. Andrew stood by Pierre.

"And Happy New Year, Uncle!" called Andrew, sounding angry.

Pierre pulled up the rope and closed the trapdoor.

"We'll be two swamp rats forever," said Andrew.

"If we live that long," Pierre said. "What if Lafitte finds out and comes after the gems? What if Evil Eye tells about the jewels to save himself?"

chapter seventeen

In the dark of morning Pierre awoke and shook his brother. "Today or tomorrow someone must leave to travel to New Orleans and make arrangements," he said. "It's only a week until the slave auction when Isabel and Bella will be sold. Seven days away."

Andrew sat up and stared at him.

"There's one person we haven't tried," said Pierre, folding his arms. "Why not tell the priest?"

Leaping to his feet, Andrew all but danced a jig. "Of course," he said, "we tell the priest. He can advise us in the confessional. If he doesn't wish to help us, he can't break the secrecy of the confessional. He can never tell!"

"Did you hear him that night?" Pierre asked.

"Sure. He covered our escape the night the *Carolina* was burning. He said he knew us." Andrew splashed water on his face and hands.

They raced to dress in clean brown outfits.

"It's our last hope. Shall we travel by day or night?" asked Pierre.

Gator Bait held both hands up. "I don't think we have a choice. We start now."

Carrying a loaf of bread and some cattail roots, they poled the boat off to a racing start. As they left, Pierre heard the owls flap and glide home from their nightly hunt. He nodded a silent greeting. He loved Monsieur and Madame Owl.

In less than five hours the brothers reached the stream where ships sailed. Around them in the mist they heard grunted commands and whispered orders for ship repairs. Sailors hammered nails; bayonets gave off sparks as soldiers sharpened them on stones. Pierre smelled cedar wood and black tar for sealing ships.

"They're preparing for the next battle," Andrew said.

Pierre didn't answer. All he could think about was whether the priest would help them. Who would go buy Isabel and Bella? Should they mention the trunk of Napoleon's treasure to the priest?

This was the second of January. The auction was on the ninth. Slave traders who purchased slaves in New Orleans took them north and sold them all along the East Coast. If Isabel and Bella were sold again, they might never be found.

Take courage, Pierre thought. Over and over he repeated it in his mind. "Gator Bait," he said, "we have courage and hope on our side. That's what Isabel would say."

Andrew nodded and pushed with his pole. "We do have courage and hope," he repeated.

When they arrived at the riverbank, Pierre ached all over. Never had they poled their boat so fast. Fortunately the day was overcast, the air cold, and fog lingered to hide them from reward-greedy eyes.

After they tied the boat beneath the riverbank overhang, they climbed up. Pierre felt pleased that the cave was nearby for refuge. Their rope still hung in the entrance.

"We can knock on the rectory door and ask for confession," said Andrew.

Suppose the priest isn't in? Pierre thought. Then someone else will know about us. He said, "Let's visit the church and pray for help."

"Good," said Andrew. "The priest might be there."

Pierre had scarcely bent his head to pray in the front of the chilly stone-walled church when his brother tugged on his hood. The two moved to the rear of the church where the priest was praying in a pew.

"*Père*, could you hear our confession?" asked Andrew in a church whisper.

This was the first time Pierre had seen the face of the priest. He was younger than Pierre had thought he would be, and slender under his loose black cassock. His dark hair was cut at ear length, and brown eyes crinkled in a well-tanned face.

"I can see why they call you the ghost-eye twins," said the priest softly, as he led them to a damp stone-box confessional. He entered the center booth; Pierre stepped behind the maroon velvet curtain on one side, and Andrew stepped in with him.

"You're supposed to go on the other side," said Pierre, pushing his brother with his elbow.

"I can come in here if I want," Andrew said, and shoved Pierre to share the kneeling pad.

Time passed in silence. Was the priest still alive? After about twenty minutes, the priest slid open the speaking door of the confessional. "Yes, my sons."

"*Père,*" said Andrew, "we need help. Our mother is being sold at the slave auction by the Bienvieux Brothers on the ninth of January."

"We want to buy her lawfully, *Père,*" said Pierre, "but of course we don't have any money or gold." Already he had a sinking feeling. Should they tell about the jewels? No.

"And we're wanted as escaped slaves ourselves, *Père,*" Andrew said. "I stole a pirate telescope. We could have stolen gold doubloons, but the pirates have hidden them." Pierre felt impatient with his brother. Why had Andrew mentioned the doubloons?

Through the screen of the confessional, Pierre saw the priest flash a smile. His teeth were moon white against his tan skin.

"Is that all?" the priest asked. His voice was patient. Head bent, he leaned forward to hear their whispers.

"My brother stole some chickens, but I returned them," Andrew said. Pierre hit him with his fist, and Andrew pushed him back. Pierre was furious. How dare Andrew lie and say he had stolen the chickens! Taking those chickens was Andrew's idea.

The priest asked again, "Is that all?"

"Oh, no," said Pierre, frowning at his brother. "We want Isabel Alexandre—our mother—and our three-year-old little sister, and all of the other seventy-two slaves we could set free."

"What he's saying, *Père*," added Andrew, "is that we want family. Our father. . . ." He stopped.

Pierre nodded. This was the confessional, with its seal of secrecy. The priest couldn't tell anything they said. Just to be certain no one was nearby, he flicked the curtain open and glanced around. He nodded to Andrew.

"Our father was Black Jack the pirate," said Andrew softly.

"His real name was Jacques Alexandre, and his half brother is a pirate named Evil Eye Alex, but he won't help us." Pierre took a deep breath. "They were sons of the Prince of Burgundy, Andrew Pierre Alexandre, our grandfather. And we don't think he would help."

Andrew said, "But we're sure the Marquis François Jean Claude De Ville wants us back as slaves. We danced and entertained his friends. And that's all, *Père*."

The priest covered a smile. "My sons," he began, "do you attend Mass faithfully?"

Pierre was startled. What did the priest mean?

"Yes, *Père*," Andrew said. "Every Sunday when we were with the Marquis De Ville, and sometimes my brother went weekdays with Aunt Berniece. That's why he doesn't like robbing pirates."

Another smile flashed. "Then, my sons, you must know that with God all things are possible."

"Really?" asked Andrew, and his voice squeaked in surprise.

Pierre elbowed his brother. "Yes, *Père*." But he

thought: This priest must be younger than he looks. Even I know how unfair life is.

The priest gave them absolution and a blessing, then said, "Come with me."

Should they trust him? Pierre wondered. Or was the priest about to capture them for the reward?

chapter eighteen

The priest led them to the side door of the church, then quickly backed away. He signaled for them to lean against the church's stone wall. When an elderly woman had limped past, he waved for them to follow him.

Hoods over faces, the boys followed the priest on a brick path to his rectory. He started for the door in front, hesitated and, turning, led them to the red door in the back facing the river.

Once inside the house, the priest spoke cheerfully to his housekeeper in the kitchen and waved the boys past. At another door he exchanged low greetings and entered. The room was dark, its drapes pulled across the windows.

"Gentlemen, forgive our intrusion, but these young boys have a problem of immense importance." Crossing the room, *Père* Simone opened the black velvet drapes.

Pierre blinked in the sudden light. The room had two tall men sitting at a bare table in the center of the room. High-back chairs lined the plastered white walls. Besides the long table and the chairs, the room was bare. Cold. Bleak.

"I know these young men," said General Andrew Jackson, resting an arm on the table.

Although Pierre had never seen the other man at ground level, he knew it was Jean Lafitte, pirate captain of the Brotherhood.

Lafitte wore no beard, but his black mustache hung in a long curl on either side of his face. He was dressed all in black. Jewelry flashed from his ears, from around his neck on many chains, and from both wrists. A sword with ruby-encrusted hilt was bound at his side.

The pirate chieftain scratched and scowled like a man irritated by fleas. Pierre wanted to cross himself, but dared not; he said a prayer. The brown mother dog lay peacefully by Lafitte's chair.

"I thought I was here to plan a battle," roared Captain Lafitte. "Away with these sniveling hen-hearted puppies!"

He tossed a dagger on the table. It stuck upright.

Mouth open, Andrew stared at the dagger, but Pierre had to keep himself from smiling. He remembered Evil Eye saying he wore an eye patch to strike terror. Jean Lafitte was only trying to frighten them. The brown dog rolled on its side.

The priest nodded for Pierre to speak. He seemed to read their different reactions to Lafitte. Pierre stood straight, head high, hands loose at his sides.

With a deep breath he said: "We need to free our mother and little sister. They are to be sold at auction January ninth at Bienvieux Brothers in New Orleans. Besides them, we want the rest of the seventy-two slaves freed." Plantation owners and slave traders bought many slaves, why shouldn't he?

Lafitte threw back his head and roared in coarse

laughter. It was a pirate laugh, loud and crude. Andrew, Pierre saw, had begun to tremble. This was his high-spirited brother who had assembled a skeleton on an island with two sleeping pirates! Why was he frightened now?

To loosen his brother, Pierre swung his arms and did a cross step. Andrew copied him and closed his mouth. It was a dance step they agreed to whenever they forgot the dance. Pierre knew Andrew understood.

See, thought Pierre, we know how to fight this battle of wills. Without blinking he looked Captain Lafitte in the eye.

"What power do you have?" asked Jean Lafitte, in a roar like a bull. He pointed at Andrew to answer. Pierre closed his eyes, then opened them quickly.

"Power?" asked Andrew in a squeaky voice. "Power? Well, we have courage and hope, sir."

General Jackson slapped the table. "That's the spirit! I want you young men for my troops in a few years." He rubbed hands together. "But," said the general in softer tones, "we must return to tactics of this great battle. Enough with the boys, Father." He waved both hands to dismiss the three of them. "If the States lose this war, we'll lose our freedom. We could lose our independence from Great Britain."

The priest spoke slowly. "The boys have a battle too. Theirs is a struggle for freedom, for independence, for family."

General Jackson frowned.

"Lafitte," asked the priest, "are your men powerful enough to steal slaves from that auction warehouse?"

"Of course," said Lafitte, with a flourish that jangled bracelets and flashed gold, "we can do anything we wish. New Orleans is a city under my very thumb."

"And under my martial laws," said the general. "But," and the general stopped, "why should I help these boys? I'm here to plan other battles, begging your pardon, Father."

"You should help us because we helped you, sir," said Pierre quickly. "We saved some of your troops."

Andrew spoke up. "How many men did we save from drowning and alligators for you, sir?" Pierre could have cheered. He and Andrew were a team in more than dance!

"Fifteen," said the general.

Pierre's mouth flew open. General Jackson had counted them? He had no idea it was that many American soldiers. He said, "Then you owe us our mother, sister, and other slaves our mother will choose. Up to fifteen, sir."

General Jackson turned. "Lafitte," he asked, "how long would it take to bring fifteen slaves here for a family for the boys of courage?"

"No time at all," said the pirate chief. "I have a chain of men who would pass word to New Orleans, and the Brotherhood would capture them from Bienvieux Brothers' warehouse. Then they would sail down the Mississippi. . . ." He stopped.

"Wait," he yelled, "I deal in slaves! From ship to shore! We rob slave traders' ships and sell onshore at lower prices. A fourth of the Brotherhood are Africans, and they don't mind selling their brethren as slaves. What am I doing helping slaves escape?"

No one spoke.

Captain Lafitte stood and folded his arms. In a roar like mild thunder he said, "I owe you numskull knaves nothing!"

Unblinking, Pierre stared him down. He was waiting for the right moment.

No one spoke.

Lafitte threw up both hands. Pierre noticed that he had all his fingers. "You chicken-hearted rascals! What do I get out of this?"

Pierre felt this was the moment. "We have something for you, sir," he said, and swung his arms to dance a cross step. Andrew understood. He copied Pierre's step. Now how best to tell the pirate chief that they had his precious jewels?

chapter nineteen

Pierre never thought faster in his life. He had to make up a story that didn't involve Black Jack or Evil Eye Alex in case Jacques—Black Jack—was still alive. He didn't want Lafitte to blame and murder either one of them.

"Sir," he began, "we found a pile of jewels."

Lafitte swung around to stare at him. His necklaces clinked, his bracelets tinkled, and his earrings flashed gold.

"They were in a house in the swamp, sir," said Andrew.

So far, so good. Pierre took a deep breath. "We noticed a French pattern. There are gem settings of diamonds in *fleur-de-lis*—lily flowers—and rubies in crowns." Quoted straight from Evil Eye himself.

With a roar Lafitte drew his sword and crossed the room in a bound. Holding the sword to Pierre's throat, he asked in a snake hiss, "Who stole my treasure?"

The priest's hand was on Pierre's shoulder. The well-sharpened sword was inches from his skin. Pierre stared at the pirate chieftain, glad *Père* Simone and Andrew were on either side of him.

"I don't know, sir," he said. "But we have a sack. We'll gather the gems and give them back to you."

Andrew added: "When we have Isabel, our little sister, and thirteen other slaves."

Pierre couldn't believe that Andrew had said that. His courage had returned if he dared bargain with Captain Jean Lafitte! It was daring, but it might also be smart. Pierre hoped the trunk was still there.

Wouldn't it be terrible if Evil Eye had dumped it in the swamp? Or had told someone about it, and that person had come to steal it? Then he and Andrew couldn't deliver after promising the pirate they would.

Pierre tried not to show worry. The pirate hadn't said anything. The sword hung in midair now.

Père Simone spoke up. "Then it's all settled. I am your go-between. When the boys bring the gems to my sacristy, I'll keep them locked up until their mother and the others are delivered."

His hands on their shoulders, the priest pulled the boys toward the door behind them. Pierre was relieved, astonished. Would it be that simple? They turned and began walking away.

"No!" shouted Jean Lafitte with a curse. "I'm not finished with these crafty sniveling rascals." Pierre turned and stared again. Would the pirate go back on the priest's arrangements?

"You're right, Jean," said General Jackson, striking the table with his fist. Turning his back to the pirate, he winked at the twins.

"We can't allow you boys to get away this easy. We demand service from you. What can you twins do to help us fight the redcoats?"

Pierre felt his knees go to jelly. How could they help in a war? From the corner of his eye, though, he saw Andrew's face light up. His brother would probably love to fight.

The general pointed to them. "You can ram powder and fill muskets for the gunners."

"Sir," said Pierre, "there's a reward out for us. The Marquis De Ville wants us back as escaped slaves. We dare not go around people." Would his excuse be strong enough?

"And we can serve you better in another way," Andrew said.

"Yes?" asked the general.

"We know of a perch high in a cypress giant in the swamp. From there we can see for miles. We can signal when the British are coming."

Nodding, Pierre said, "We can use fire."

Patting their backs, the priest walked out and returned in seconds with a covered lantern. "This is a special signal lantern," he said, "the type they use in lighthouses." He showed them how to light it.

The general pointed. "Perfect. Father, show them how to raise and lower the shutter for the signal."

"Tomorrow night we can practice," said Andrew. "We'll flash twice."

"And we'll return it, won't we, Lafitte?" asked the general.

The pirate glanced back and forth from the boys to the general. He frowned at the priest, rubbed his chin, twirled his long, stiff mustache.

"Other swamp dwellers signal with lanterns. How will I know your signal?" General Jackson asked.

Pierre said, "We'll flash fifteen times for the fifteen

slaves to be freed. As soon as we see the British moving, we'll flash. No other swamp people will flash that many times."

"Fifteen it is," said the general.

With a loud snarl, Jean Lafitte swung his sword and cut in two a black velvet drape at the window. "Who are these knaves, these scoundrels, to bargain with me? I am Jean Lafitte!"

The priest smiled. "Who are they? Don't you understand, Jean?" He waved a hand to include all of them. "We're all God's children!"

He picked up the cut piece of velvet. "And I want another drape, thank you, Jean. No. A matching set, any dark color." He opened the door, and he and the twins walked out.

He whispered to them, "You'll bring the jewels to me? In a bag?" Hoods pulled, they stood in shadows by the rectory door. Pierre nodded and prayed those gems were still there.

"Where do we leave the sack, *Père?*" asked Andrew.

"I'll put a chair behind the altar," said the priest. He put arms around their shoulders. "Do you see this face?"

Pierre stared at the well-tanned face of the young priest, the straight black hair, the smiling brown eyes, and full lips.

"I too am of African ancestry, and no one knows. Take courage and put your hope in God!"

It was late in the foggy afternoon when they began the return trip to Hôtel de Jacques. Andrew stopped on the way to pluck a supply of snails, and he caught a catfish for a boiled fish feast. When they reached Hôtel de Jacques at midnight, Andrew turned to Pierre.

"How are fifteen people going to live here?"

Pierre hadn't even thought of that. He raised his hands. "Since the impossible might happen," he told his brother, "the possible can be worked out later."

The first thing he did was check Jacques's trunk. It was still full of gems. "I can't believe we did it," he said.

The following night they flashed twice from the third-floor room and saw a return flash from the earthworks. After that, the next two days they were busy. Day and night they took four-hour turns watching the British.

"They're still busy repairing ships," said Andrew finally. "Why not take the jewels now?"

Pierre put all the jewels in their chicken sack. In the dark of night they poled their pirogue and delivered the sack to the chair behind the altar. As they crept away, the priest waved in passing from the rectory. They knew he would take the sack.

When they returned to Hôtel de Jacques, the British still had not moved. For two more days the redcoats brought big guns into the swampland. However, on the evening of January seventh, the British ships and longboats were unusually still. The rising moon was bright.

"Should we signal?" asked Pierre.

"Not until they begin sailing."

They slept in turns and kept watch well into the night. In the middle of the night Andrew dropped from the third story. "Wake up, Pierre. They're moving. The British are moving."

"Where's the lantern?" Pierre called. He felt frantic.

Andrew had jumped down the ladder. "Here," he passed it up from the first floor. His hands were shaking. The lantern had sat in the damp air, and water droplets rolled along the glass.

Pierre opened the firebox. "Here's the flame."

Andrew touched the wet lantern wick to their firebox flame, and the fire went out. The room was dark black.

"Where is it?" Pierre asked. His voice squeaked.

"Out! What do you think?" Andrew yelled, stomping his foot. "*Sacré bleu!* You did it. You should have covered that lantern. It's soaked in dew!"

Pierre felt angry. If the lantern was wet with dew, Andrew was to blame as well. It looked as if they couldn't warn the Americans!

chapter twenty

How can we start a new fire?" Pierre called. His hands shook so badly he almost dropped the lantern. "All these weeks and our fire never went out before."

"We can strike stones," Andrew called, "set the dry cattail straw afire."

"What stones?"

Without answering, Andrew dropped from the first floor to the cypress knees to feel around for a stone in the water.

"Watch out for Dagger-tooth," called Pierre.

He longed for one of the stones from the cave. He remembered the rope and stone he had thrown for his brother to climb out of the Cajun's cabin.

"A snail shell," he called, as he set the lantern down. "Andrew, come back. Help me dry a snail shell."

Dripping wet and shivering, Andrew climbed up on the rope. "I couldn't find a stone down there."

They tried scratching snail shells with no luck. "Jacques's sword and dagger," said Pierre. "We'll strike them together."

As Pierre struck metal together again and again,

Andrew climbed back to the third story to stare. Already they had wasted about an hour.

"The British ships are near the earthworks, but in that low mist the Americans will never see them," he called. "Hurry!"

"Help me if you want me to hurry!"

They drew a spark, but it hissed out. The straw they uncovered had become damp from the night's dew. They drew more sparks. Soon the straw began to smoke. Pierre blew it gently. It crackled and spit. Andrew fanned the tiny flame until they had a small fire. Pierre held the fire to the damp lantern wick. It smoldered, then caught and flared brilliantly. Lantern in hand, Andrew climbed up to the lookout.

Pierre counted as his brother flashed fifteen times. A single blink answered them.

"Hurry," called Andrew. "We'll take the boat and get closer." Pierre nodded. He hated battles, but he felt a part of this one.

It took four hours for the twins to pole their pirogue close to the earthworks. When they were at a safe distance, they tied their boat near a cypress and climbed up.

For the next hour they sat together waiting. Besides the ship's telescope, Andrew had brought cattails and snails to eat. They sipped water.

"When are they going to begin?" Pierre asked.

Daylight had begun to wash the sky in the east. "It's too bright now," said Andrew. "Maybe the British will wait another day."

Pierre pointed. "No. More British troops are sailing in."

In a moment, the British ships fired cannon and muskets at the earthworks. Pierre dreaded the battle, but he also wanted it over with. He could imagine how the men behind the earthworks were feeling. The British ships kept firing, but the Americans didn't answer fire.

"What're they doing?" asked Pierre, clasping his hands. "What's the trouble? Didn't they see our signal?"

"See our signal?" Andrew called, holding the telescope. "They're under fire now. Who needs a signal?"

The British stopped firing.

All around them it grew dark. The sun was covered by a cloak of gray clouds, and a heavy fog rolled in from the Gulf. Now the brothers saw only gray.

"Are they still there?" asked Pierre in a whisper.

Andrew shrugged and sat staring. Pierre climbed down and cut cattails from the boat for a couple of hours. He couldn't sit still. At mid-morning a sudden breeze cleared the fog.

"Come up," Andrew shouted. "Look at this!"

In front of the earthworks on a bend of land, Pierre saw a moving mass of red. Bayonets shone like diamond tips over ruby-red jackets.

"Where are the Americans?" Andrew asked, staring through his telescope at the earthworks. He handed the telescope to Pierre.

"Maybe they withdrew. I can't see any men or guns."

"Look how many troops the British have," Andrew said.

Pierre stared through the telescope. "The Americans don't have half that many." He grasped a tree branch. "This could be awful."

The mass of red moved forward like stinging red ants from an anthill. Finally the American cannons fired through the earthworks. Then rifles shot at the British, followed by muskets opening fire.

From their perch, Pierre saw red uniforms crumple, redcoat soldiers topple. The British returned fire, but the redcoats kept falling over each other. In a short time the heaps of British soldiers were deathly still.

Andrew called, "I think I see a British soldier with a white flag." Soon all firing ceased. All the while the Americans were hidden behind their wall of earth.

Pierre felt sick over so many dead soldiers. That afternoon he and Andrew watched British soldiers digging huge trenches. Bodies still in bright uniforms were rolled into the open trenches used as graves. Climbing down, the twins poled their boat back to Hôtel de Jacques.

The next day longboats began carrying the wounded British soldiers and sailors. Some were moaning, others were shrieking; the cries carried well across the swamp waters.

The cries of the wounded quieted the songbirds. Turtles seemed to draw their heads into their shells. Snakes coiled in silence. Ducks and geese floating on the waters drew closer together. Pierre felt that their owl neighbors fluffed their feathers higher and buried their heads deeper under their wings.

He supposed the Battle of New Orleans was over; he supposed the Americans had won.

The next few days he and Andrew went about washing, fishing, and harvesting cattails, wild onions, and garlic.

Their green kingdom returned to hoarse honks of geese, frog chirps, and quacking flocks of wintering ducks. The boys had done all they could.

Would General Andrew Jackson and Captain Jean Lafitte keep their end of the bargain? Pierre and Andrew had signaled before the battle. And surely the priest had told the pirate chief that he had the precious French jewels.

"Suppose they do get freed," said Andrew one morning. "Where are they going to live? You asked for fifteen slaves to be freed. How are you going to feed them? Where will they sleep?"

"We'll find a way," Pierre said. "First, we see if they free Isabel and the others. We have to wait."

"You *are* weak," said Andrew. "The marquis was right. All you do is wait." He stuck out his tongue at Pierre and climbed to the third story.

Pierre winced. Sometimes living with Andrew was like living with a sputtering cannon.

The next evening Andrew fell asleep early. Pierre sat staring at the misty air. Andrew's taunt rang in his ears. *You are weak. All you do is wait.*

That wasn't exactly true. Who had rescued Andrew? That night he had poled the pirogue many miles by himself. Could he do it again?

Suppose he asked *Père* Simone about a place to live with his family? The priest called the pirate chieftain by his first name. Pirates traveled the swamplands and knew the islands best. The priest might be able to ask Jean Lafitte about a place to live. Anyway, it was worth a try.

Pierre slid over to the creaking ladder and stepped

down slowly. He would go and ask. The swamplands were safe to travel in now. I am not weak, he thought. I'll show Andrew.

Taking rope, water, and cattail roots, he swung to the hidden pirogue. He waved good-bye to Dagger-tooth and set off.

Eleven hours later he climbed back into Hôtel de Jacques and rolled in his blanket to sleep. At daybreak Andrew nudged him with his foot.

"Wake up."

Pierre turned over. "I want to sleep."

"Well, it's time to get up."

Should he tell Andrew? No. Besides, would his twin believe him if he did tell? Pierre yawned and returned to sleep.

The next few days Pierre felt as if he were walking around holding his breath. Andrew had stopped speaking to him and seldom helped him around Hôtel de Jacques. Waiting seemed unbearable. The January days grew colder and colder. I must be patient, Pierre thought.

One morning Andrew coiled rope and filled a bag with cattail roots. "Come on," he said.

Pierre sat washing clothes. "Where to?" he asked. Andrew was so bored with waiting that he wanted to go exploring? Well, sometimes people just had to wait. Pierre had done all he could. He wanted to be at Hôtel de Jacques when they brought his mother and sister there, but how would the pirates know where to find them?

Andrew said, "Let's go see if the pirates are still on their island. I bet we could live on that island. Or we could live in the cave. I can't just sit here. Come on, Pierre."

Pierre took a deep breath. "Go ahead," he said. "I don't think it's wise to leave. I'm not going anywhere." He had spoken softly, but his heart hammered loudly in his chest.

"Come on, Pierre. Hen Heart! We can't just sit here waiting. In the pirogue we can travel fast." Andrew nodded. "Let's see what those pirates are up to."

Climbing to the top room, Pierre began hanging a washed green jacket to dry. It blended with the tree. "No, Andrew."

He felt a thump and almost fell from the tree. His brother had thrown a coil of rope at his back. Swirling around, he returned it, throwing it into his brother's face.

Andrew fell on his back and lay staring at him. "Pierre," he said, "Aunt Berniece told you to take care of me."

Pierre took green trousers and another jacket. He said nothing as he crawled farther out to hang them.

"Well," called Andrew, "I'm going."

For a while his brother bustled about on the first floor. Pierre kept listening. Andrew had never traveled in the boat without him, but he, Pierre, had made two round trips alone. Pierre held his breath. Soon Andrew climbed back up and threw the rope in a corner. Pierre let out his breath.

No longer would he allow his twin to rule his life. When Andrew's plans made sense, he would join him. Otherwise, he was an independent boy!

A week later they awoke to tapping. Pierre ran down to stare out the wall. Evil Eye, standing in a longboat, was tapping with an oar.

"Boys," he called, "come join your mother and family. Captain Lafitte says you have his permission to live on Grand Terre Island. We pirates won't be needing it. With our pardons, we can live anywhere we want to."

Pierre grinned at Andrew. Grand Terre Island? A place to live, and he had helped arrange it! The priest had done what he promised. Now they had both family and a home!

The pirate flashed a smile. "There, no one will dare capture you. Jean Lafitte's name will protect you!" Mist swirled around Evil Eye's purple trousers, and he had pushed his eye patch high.

"Isabel?" Pierre asked, rubbing his eyes. He shivered in his underwear. It seemed so early in the morning.

"And little Jacqueline, along with thirteen others. Jean Lafitte is a man of his word!" Evil Eye chuckled. "You'll be quite an addition to the dozen or so people on the island!"

So her name was Jacqueline, not Bella. Named after Jacques.

In a flurry the twins dressed and packed. Andrew gathered clothes, and Pierre stored tools and rope, pots and pans in the trunk. He covered it with a cloak. In less than an hour he and Andrew lowered their bags and trunk into the longboat.

Before he left, Pierre set his two grinning skulls to guard Hôtel de Jacques. One skull sat by the door on the first story, and the other on the second story.

After tying their pirogue to the longboat, Andrew helped Evil Eye row. Glancing around, Pierre bid silent farewell to Dagger-tooth and to Monsieur and Madame

Owl. He wished he could take the owls with him, but his owls were wild free birds, and Pierre respected freedom. The fog lifted as they rowed toward a small sailing ship with sharply pointed bow and stern.

From the distance he saw black men and women royally dressed in reds, greens, golds, blues.

"Where did they get the clothes?" asked Andrew.

"Compliments of Captain Lafitte," said their uncle.

From that distance Pierre couldn't tell where Isabel was. He kept staring until he spied her waving. He thought she looked thinner than she had before. The little girl in her arms was pretty as a sunrise, with a head full of black curls, rosy cheeks, and gray eyes.

Pierre tapped Andrew's shoulder and held his arms open. The twins hugged, pushed apart, and hugged again. "We did it," Pierre said. Andrew nodded. He seemed close to tears.

When they climbed the rope ladder to the deck, Isabel smothered them with kisses. Jacqueline held her mother's long blue skirt and hid her face shyly.

"Oh, my sons," Isabel said, sobbing, "we're together at last!"

Shortly after they boarded, the ship set sail. Andrew talked to his mother, telling her everything. Pierre wanted to ask her some questions, but Andrew held his mother's arm and shut Pierre out of the conversation.

Looking at his twin, Pierre shook his head. Andrew is still Andrew, he thought. Pierre couldn't change his brother, but he had changed himself.

They had different talents, different strengths, different weaknesses. He had to admit that without his brother, he wouldn't have survived, and wouldn't have been able to free Isabel, Jacqueline, and the other slaves. But without him, Andrew would not have survived either.

Differences were good. Together they made a great team.

Glancing around, Pierre noticed about half of the slaves were men, and half were women. Of African ancestry, but racially mixed, their skin colors varied. Some were black, some brown, some ivory tan. Many stood in family groups with infants. They would be a wonderful colony, a big family!

Pierre took little Jacqueline's hand, and they sat by the rail. He snapped his fingers to call one of the pirate puppies. Two of the three fluffy brown puppies were there, but the mother dog was missing. Pierre supposed it was with the pirate chief.

Pierre held the soft puppy to his cheek. "See the little puppy?" he asked Jacqueline.

His uncle walked over. "Want it?" asked Evil Eye.

Pierre nodded, and Jacqueline called, "Yes. My puppy!"

Hugging the puppy and Jacqueline, Pierre asked her, "Don't you think Grateful would be a nice name for our puppy?"

"Yes, Pierre. I love that name." She pulled his head down and kissed her brother on his cheek.

That evening in an early January sunset, the pirates landed all the freed slaves on the lush, tropical island of

Grand Terre. Pirates stood with arms folded. Pierre wondered if they had enjoyed doing something worthwhile for a change.

As the freed slaves climbed down and waded ashore, they called thanks and farewell. Women carrying infants left first, then other women and men followed.

Last of all the twins climbed down the ship's rope ladder. Evil Eye leaned near and whispered to his nephews: "Any coward can rob and kill, but to care takes courage!"

Author's Note

The War of 1812 between America and Great Britain ended with the Peace of Christmas Eve, 1814. However, news of the end of the war did not reach New Orleans until the middle of February 1815. In December 1814, the British chose to attack beautiful New Orleans where twenty-five thousand people lived. Produce and merchandise had been blockaded in port, and seizing this "booty" appealed to the British. Their watchword and countersign were, "Beauty and booty."

The British offered thirty thousand pounds to Captain Jean Lafitte and his pirate Brotherhood who terrorized the Gulf Coast. They needed the help of the pirates in the unknown wetlands southeast of the city. The vengeful pirates' sea fortress on Grand Terre Island had been fired on by the American navy in September 1814.

However, for a legal pardon from piracy laws, Jean Lafitte offered to aid the Americans instead of the British. General Andrew Jackson accepted help from the pirates. He made Jean Lafitte his unofficial *aide-de-camp*, and the pirates helped him prepare for the Battle of New Orleans.

The general called the pirates "hellish banditti" but

needed men, artillery, and ammunition from the Brotherhood. Besides, the colorful pirates were excellent artillerymen and knew the local wetlands.

A son of Jacques Villeré escaped and told the Americans when the British made their headquarters at Villeré's plantation on Pea Island in the swampland east of New Orleans. At seven-thirty P.M. on December 23, 1814, two American ships, the fourteen-gun *Carolina* and the twenty-two-gun *Louisiana,* fired on the British headquarters, catching them by surprise. By Christmas Day the British brought in four thousand soldiers from ships.

Meanwhile, General Jackson's American forces built an earthworks between a cypress swamp on the east and the Mississippi River on the west.

On December 28, 1814, the British attacked the *Carolina* and *Louisiana,* and the *Carolina* caught fire. On December 31, the British fired from heavy guns hidden behind sugar casks on their ships. They presumed sugar would protect their gunners as casks of sand did, but they were mistaken. American fire dismantled the guns and killed the gunners.

On January 8, 1815—the date of the Battle of New Orleans—the British wanted to attack in the dark, but started to attack nearer daylight. In thick fog British soldiers landed and marched. When the fog lifted, British troops had marched close to the Americans. American fighters hidden behind their earthworks were French, Spanish, Native Americans, English, and African Americans from New Orleans and Santo Domingo. They held their fire while the British marched closer and closer.

At five hundred yards American soldiers fired cannons; at three hundred yards riflemen fired; at one hundred yards soldiers with muskets opened fire. Even for British veterans of the Napoleonic wars, the grapeshot and canister fire were devastating. The dead and wounded lay in heaps of scarlet-and-white uniforms. The British lost about two thousand men; the Americans lost seventy, and only thirteen Americans died on General Jackson's side of the river.

The British hoisted a white flag of defeat. They dug trenches to serve as common graves, and they rolled their dead soldiers and sailors into those graves. The most successful battle for America in the War of 1812 was over.

The contribution of Jean Lafitte and his pirate Brotherhood was great. Following Jackson's promise, the Louisiana legislature asked for a pardon for all the pirates. President James Madison did pardon them. However, many of the Brotherhood returned to piracy. Jean Lafitte was reported killed in a fight with a British sloop-of-war in 1823.

The pirates' fortress island of Grand Terre is present on old maps, but is missing on recent maps because a hurricane destroyed the island. The smaller pirates' island the twins visited might have been one of many in the swamps.

Our ghost-eye twins, Pierre and Andrew Alexandre, had their purpose and struggles and lived in fiction in the midst of this last battle of the War of 1812. May we all "take courage" from their story.

Bibliography

Gosse, Philip. *The History of Piracy*. New York: Tudor Publishing Company, 1934.

Hickey, Donald R. *The War of 1812: A Forgotten Conflict*. Illinois: University of Illinois Press, 1989.

Hoppe, E. O. *Pirates, Buccaneers, and Gentlemen Adventurers*. London: A. S. Barnes and Company, Inc., 1972.

Niering, William A., editor. *Wetlands. Audubon Society Nature Guide*. New York: Alfred A. Knopf, Inc., 1985.

Pirates of the Spanish Main. By editors of American Heritage Magazine of History. New York: American Heritage Publishing Co., Inc., 1961.

Rankin, Hugh F. *The Golden Age of Piracy*. Williamsburg, Virginia: Colonial Williamsburg, Inc., 1969.

Ward, Ralph T. *Pirates in History*. Baltimore: York Press, Inc., 1974.